The Horse of Selene

by Juanita Casey

Horse by the River. *poems*

Juanita Casey

The Horse of Selene

The Dolmen Press
London: Calder and Boyars

Set in Times Roman type and printed and
published in the Republic of Ireland
by the Dolmen Press Limited
8 Herbert Place Dublin 2.

Distributed outside Ireland, except in the U.S.A.
and in Canada by Calder and Boyars Limited
18 Brewer Street London W1R 4A5

First published 1971

SBN 85105 187 1

© Juanita Casey 1971

Although they may be in the wind,
the way legends are; told, yet familiar to us
even untold, these events may or may not
be in our time.
But they have been, and they will be to come.
Until there are no more men nor women,
And no more horses.

There had always been horses on the island, a wandering fluid band which had additions at times when a pony broke its hobbles and was away to them, and no-one bothered to go and catch it when an ass is better, all told. Or the tinkers' piebalds would join them, and these being usually entires it was pretty sure next year there'd be some magpie foals with some of the mares. Ponies, a couple of cart-horses, and a few good lookers, all as unkempt and wild as mountainy ewes, and all colours.

Death took away from them too, but mostly the body lay where it fell, for it is a great business burying a horse, and the dogs of the island would eat their owners should they fall down. Often the beast would lie strangely by the sea's edge, with the head stretched out on the tide as though it could see some great land afar off, or one of the colts could not meet the cruelties of winter.

Their leaders changed too; sometimes a gaunt old mare, sometimes a cocky stallion.

A dun left behind still some of his wily breed which are good for anything and indestructible in the heart. A black with a head like a currach one year, and this time a white, a true white with a pretty way of going and a tail he held up like a gale warning.

They looked grand when lit by the sun, or drinking in the lake of an evening when the swans creamed down on the dark water to take their night's rest, but most thought the horses were a nuisance, a danger, and not what you wished your daughter to see when some damned stallion began his stuff right outside your front windows, and, seeing few houses had fences, often right on your very doorstep.

They trampled the island gardens, broke down walls, splintered fences, ate washing and at times terrorised strangers with teeth and bullying.

7

The worst thing was the harm they did in the grave-yard, to which they were irresistably drawn by its lush grass, and if not seen in time and driven out they would doze propped against the headstones, or lie on a newly dug mound and roll in its flowers, and the great rubbery farts they let out were enough to wake the poor defiled dead themselves.

As likely as not they are Godless; without their God and therefore without hope of grace or fortune in this world or the next.

Father Muldoon was hot on his favourite scent, a bloodhound of righteousness diligently nosing out the impurities of his congregation and chopping at them with flews smacking and as much spit as a curbed horse, with his Mayo brogue rising as he cornered and shook their iniquities one by one on a fine Sunday morning.

For the season of the cars and the caravans was on; over the hills the tourists crawled and dipped, the students padded, the Americans gawped, swivelling their cameras in a frenzy to record every moment of their fishbowl tour, the caravans bumped along the gritty tracks and the tents flowered all over the island as though the rains brought them up overnight. The English men subdued the lakes with flailing rods and prickly hats, and their bored wives tried to appear unconcerned at the avid eyes consuming them to the bone from every side. The tinkers ran their feet off and exhausted their repertoire of disasters for extracting sympathy at its best, money. The tourists, the guests, the visitors, the bloody foreigners arrived in Aranchilla as the cuckoos wisely left.

These were the people Father Muldoon thundered

against at his annual verbal flagellation of the subject; most were un-Catholic, worse, atheists; these would corrupt and serpent into his flock their particular brands of temptation, their smiles hid the devil's leer if only his poor flock could see it, their radios spewed forth lewdness to which they danced and shook like savages, their young men were as ravenous for the female population of the island as savage dogs after innocent lambs — the innocent lambs shuddered with holy fear and unholy expectation — and their young women were set down upon the fair shores of Aranchilla to flaunt their shorts and uplift for the express purpose of leading the island men to whore after strange gods.

Father Muldoon's 'whore' rolled round the heads of his congregation like thunder and dogs' teeth over bones, and the male members, returning abruptly from reveries of the shorts and uplift, jumped visibly.

The tirade over, his shaken flock emerged into the sun, drawing their ordinary selves back on again like comfortable old coats, and Father Muldoon, tipping back the last measures of the altar wine, was unaware he had said 'Good luck now' to the Crucifixion as he did so.

Miceal, leaving Mass, walked slowly uphill through the white houses to the edge of the lower mountain, where the walls, which firmly kept the field patches in place, gave up the struggle and let the big stones of the mountain take over. Living alone, a further mile up the track, he took his main evening meal with his aunt's people, and Sunday dinner.

A smell of roast came down to him and he saw only the one Ulster pig which ran to meet him, then

9

turned back, keeping a squinting black look on him sideways. He wondered did he know what the smell was, that its wee brother could become in a twinkling such a savour that the mouth watered. The farm dogs sat as near the kitchen door as they could, with heads up, drawing down the goodness of it to their very ear-bones, eyes closed and noses fingering every nuance and subtlety as it wreathed round their heads like a savoury crown.

He was at the door when he thought suddenly of the girl he had seen by the strand on the night before, when taking up his five cows to their milking. Sure to God Father Muldoon's words could not be for this one; her smile had been quick and her face clear and as open as the islanders' were clouded. She had turned away to some others by the fire they had made from the furze around.

She was a student, he thought. Her hair was long and very fine he could see, and so fair it seemed almost white. He had looked away then, feeling awkward when one of the cows had streamed just by them, but they had said good evening as though it hadn't been at all. He heard them singing later, and one of their lads was playing a guitar. The tune one he didn't know.

He jabbed the nearest cow up the path to the croft, and turned to watch the cars on the white hill road running like ants down a peeled stick. It was strange how sound carried over the lake some nights. He could still hear the singing. A heron stood like a post in his usual place, and Miceal saw the swan that had lost its mate, drawn away from the others with its head coiled down its back.

God save all here; he stood in the door's arch and his aunt called from the back, Is it you Miceal. It is. Well, and if you're not the tardy one ...

10

Potatoes banged their heads on a lid and water was strained over the nettles. A cat leaped crossly for the wall as the boiling stream sidled towards him, threatening a novel neutering had it caught him where he was literally napping. Miceal stood by his place as the roast was hurried to the table, and outside, where the bent though undaunted nettles still steamed, the dogs straightened and their eyes hardened.

In the rare sunlight, the band of horses, which all that morning had delighted the visitors photographing them in statuesque poses against the dramatic scenery, and who had accepted their offerings of bread with a withdrawn thoughtfulness curiously irritating in its lack of gratitude, grazed with gritty determination among the headstones once again, snatching and roping in the grass as they expected to be chased out with the usual outrage, hurriedly sorting flowers with fumbling lips and discarding the artificial.

The big black, with the lightning blaze, rocked gently back and forth with his behind digging into the pleasantly sharp edge of a Celtic cross, and the white, raising his tail, sighed, and Mary, beloved wife of Fintan Duffy, received an unexpected tribute which would guarantee a powerful growth of grass around her for a good year.

The first ass set the doors of the morning swinging on rusty hinges; she wakened Miceal as usual. She was always the first to roar, blast her.

Uh-huh, uh-huh, it went on and on.

11

A dying Huhhhhhh, and she listened contentedly for the resultant pandemonium.

The tinkers' jack in the valley nearly split himself in answer, and immediately every contrary beast on the island honed out its challenge, greeting or lament to all the others in its hairy hierarchy. They sawed the island into chunks, and only when the last despairing chord had died away, did the returning silence help it rearrange itself again.

The mountain was unmoved; it had to be a very fine day before it took off its cap of clouds to the sun. A pair of ravens croaked to each other in familiar husband-and-wife voices as they eyed the lands below them, and planed down on the strand to see what the night's tide had left. The same heron prepared to guard his day as rigidly as he had the night, occasionally stalking out like a grey Christian Brother, to catch and chastise the young eel, swallowing him sins and all. R.I.P. and the cold yellow eye unswivelled and unrelenting.

Got ye, ye young scab.

Shrill terns eddied and blew, crouched and twinkled here and there, and the swans, feeling the chop of the dawn wind against their breasts, rose together with a carrillon of wings and beat down to the more sheltered end of the lake, turning with a quickening pulse into the wind and taking the water again, still together and with a jabot of foam at every breast.

The lonely one at first took no heed of them going, then as they cruised with heads under the shallows, he rose heavily, leaned down-wind after them and landed a distance away. In a fury of self-aggression he surged about without purpose in his frustration and loneliness, his raised wings guarding his frenzy.

Miceal's black cows lay waiting for him quietly under the wall; they had ground their night away and swallowed it, belched up the stars and swallowed them, breathed in the clouds and the mists out of their mouths, and had lain on pockets of the night wind which was easy to the bones.

They were hornless, and their black polls rose from the surrounding hair like rocks from seaweed. They breathed quietly and dozed, their fringed black eyelashes drawn over their eyes like undertakers' curtains, and one had her tail curled round like an old fashioned cream jug.

Cockerels, waiting until the ass competition was ended, saluted the dawn, the island, their wives and particularly themselves, and like the rest of the inhabitants, went back to sleep again.

Down in the tents and in the caravans, alarm clocks resounded with habit, aggravating everyone and frightening the tar-faced sheep which fled up the dunes, scattering pebbles and pellets in cross-fire panic. The one trousered goat amongst them, put there vaguely for fertility and protection, grinned to the sky unperturbed, and scratched the root of his pointed tail with one expert horn.

The wives relaxed again thankfully, some of the young men and girls strove to join interrupted episodes to the next hopeful instalment, and husbands burrowed back into sleep like puppies after milk. Only the children were up, quiet and uncertain what to do, fearing to disturb by playing too early. Three were hysterical with threatened explosion, listening by one of the caravans to a snorer with talent and variety, whose best arpeggio rose to the booming crescendo of a sea-elephant in rut.

And the horses slipped and stumbled down the shifting stones on to the white strand, where they nosed and blew over the sea-weed, bit neighbourly necks as favours granted and received, until the white horse, imagining Something beside a rock, swerved and high-tailed up the sand, cupping it away from him in quick jerks, as a stag does, head turning back, eyeing his ghost from either side and whistling nasally like a swan. The others, caught with the excuse of his assumed fears, joyfully pounded after him.

The crash of their hooves on the stones joined the roar of the surf, and the noise thundered over the tents and caravans as though the six hundred were to die again.

The call to reveille never saw so many rising so quickly as on the plains of Aranchilla.

Miceal had milked his cows; they were at leisure to go where they willed for the day, for all the beasts could roam at commonage except the asses, which being needed for the turf and aught else, hopped and curts-eyed bleakly round the homesteads, prim forelegs hobbled virginally together to prevent straying.

He stood as he always did, even when raining—which Lord alone knows was often enough — listening to the

14

island taking on the day, and watching the play beginning at every turn.

Sounds rose, though so removed from their origins that it was not easy to place them.

A dog, soundlessly barking around the heels of cows; you knew he was barking, but by the time the sound had weasled up the sides of the mountain, the barking came from an empty field, and dog and cows were up the lane and nearly home to the pail.

He saw whose fields were knitted with lain hay, whose cows, black like his own, still awaited their owners at the gates, who was it walked by the lake, who had begun to hem his handkerchief field with the plough, whose hay-cocks were safely hatted against the weather; the tinkers spreading out over the furze like rabbiting dogs gathering sticks for their day's fire, the soundless splashing of their chequered horses as one of their children in a red coat chased them back to the camp through the wet edges of the lake.

He watched, as always. He could see to the strand's edge, which had only the horses on it usually at this time, but he could see, too, that no one was yet out of the yellow and blue tent where the fair girl was. He stretched and yawned, and the collie, watching his face as a man watches weather, ran down the path, came back to see if he was following, curled up his tail like a tea-cup handle and trotted ahead with a skitter of claws on the hard white stones.

The aunt Minna was rattling around her kitchen in the flurry which still twitched her about, even though her entire family save one lad and a girl was away in England. She had been without her man, Peadar, for

15

years. The habit never left her, and she flew and
scurried from morning until nightfall, down to the
village, back up again even more pressingly as she felt
time and the incline conspirators against her, out to the
hens, here, there and all places at the same breathless
trot, and always accompanied by noise. Things fell,
were knocked over, replaced to fall again, admonished
crossly and she was sure moved again of their own
volition with the sole intention of aggravating the heart
and soul out of her. Paper of all sorts was particularly
given to treasonable activity. For her bags burst quietly
and with unseen craft, trickling away their contents out
of one corner with stealth and spite, or magnificently
and suddenly, with abandon and purpose, all over.

Newspapers were liable to fight; pages shifted from
back to front, and when replaced, some demon managed
to whisk them round upside-down. They suddenly grew
paper arms and tried to strangle her with the power
of the printed word, and lovingly clung round her feet
like a proposing lover, hobbling and finally throwing
her in a welter of market reports, Father of Nineteen
Dies Suddenly, and Girl Says She was Forced, says
Gardai.

A smiling Sister, now happily Mary Immaculate
and formerly Miss Betty O'Donnell of Letterkenny,
home on holiday for six weeks from Florida, spent it
uncomfortably wedged under one of aunt Minna's
shoes, with her smile pressed into the ragged red strip
of ancient material the aunt called me bitta Turkey,
and firmly believed it. Although at such an insult it
was a wonder it didn't up and render the whole of
Kevin Barry, seeing it came from the backs of several
County Leitrim ewes, long since martyred, and, for
once, not by the British.

Aunt Minna, getting herself and the fragments

16

together, found the Girl Forced only to take a short cut home, which was downright dishonesty and added yet another recruit to those forces designing her constant discomforture.

The deceased Father of Nineteen's obituary drew a snort and the comment No Wonder.

Peadar, good man, shifting constantly from chair, bed, table or wherever Minna ordered him as she swept, polished and besomed around him, finally shifted obediently into his grave where he could cause no more obstruction. He used to tell her that she'd surely find something undone should the Last Post sound unexpectedly and rush back, even if it meant St. Peter himself was kept waiting to lock up after the last straggler in. Being an old I.R.A. man, he slipped in an army metaphor whenever possible, to remind those all too easily forgetful of his fight for their freedom.

In fact, the only battle he'd been near was over a good hour when he arrived on a borrowed bicycle, and the only smoke rising was not from the battlefield but from the village dinners. He was wounded 'on patrol', not as he would have you believe in a glorious charge against the Saxon foe, but from a bullet accidentally fired by an unpatriotic dog tripping over his .303 while he was privately behind a bush. He had a stiffness in his gait which folk thought was his leg; only Minna and his Company knew the truth of it. Twelve-Bore Kinsella he was called from then on, the only man with two holes where most had the one. Now, his Celtic cross leaned awry away in the cemetery at the mountain's foot, worn smooth on the corners, not from pious lips but by the rubbings of horses. The big black was responsible for its Pisa, going down against it and flattening along it ecstatically as a dog goes against a fence.

The graveyard was aloof from its church and from the rest of the island, not like the Protestant church that broods her stony chicks tucked close about her.

A steep track of white stones nibbled among the boulders to it. From a distance its white headstones looked like a gardener's markers at the end of his planted rows; here lieth Forget Me Not, dearly beloved wife of Winter Broccoli. You expected a wholesale flowering, suddenly, the dead all blooming in a riot of colours, and only sour old Maguire would come up an artichoke to spoil the effect. So many of the graves were marked with the shining white quartz stones taken from the mountain, and so many of these stones still remained on it, up to the very top, like so many stars Miceal used to think them, that it was difficult to tell which were people and which was mountain, which perhaps is as it should be.

Miceal bent his head quickly and crossed himself as his path joined the track to the graveyard. His father, Patrick Kinsella, was there since a young man; Miceal could not remember him; he was taken, as were so many then, with the broken lungs. His mother too; only two years gone and now he was alone at the croft.

It seemed far longer to Miceal, set now into a steady rhythm of life like a horse ploughing.

A strong, remote woman, silent and seemingly hard, she had no time for tears, either in other people or in her own children. She had worked as hard and as long hours as a man at the tasks of the farm as well as her own, her dress long, usually grey, a handkerchief over her hair, always a large apron and a man's boots. Her hands were brown and corded, her face he remembered

18

rocky, square between the scarf's frame, the eyes a curious silver, so pale they were hardly a blue, sometimes frightening. She was thought by many to have the gift of the Sight, but this she neither affirmed nor denied, or if she knew it, had never used it for or against anyone in her lifetime.

But if she said someone was mad or a fool or good, then in spite of opposite appearances, that person was as she said, however well hidden or denied.

And if she said, unexpectedly, a horse would bolt, or Mrs. Collins would get horned soon by the cow she particularly doted on, or that striped collie was going to tear the face off the youngest Tuohy, then these things happened. Even though you would have said Lavell's old grey would no more run if you were to fire a cannon through his ears, and Mrs. Collin's cows were all her children, she never having one, and the collie had always been young Mrs. Tuohy's pet for years. But Mary Kinsella knew that Mrs. Collins would enrage her quick little cow by trying to make its calf hers too, and the striped collie, banished to the yard and neglected now that the Tuohys had their firstborn, at last would one day wreak his distress upon his innocent usurper.

And much as Mary disliked horses, which she did though she never told why, she knew them and saw them in a way which was strange, seeing that she hardly went near one.

Miceal remembered suddenly a day when she was driving in the cows for milking; two were blue then, and she was wearing a blue dress; blue sky. One cow was black, so were the two cats, the sheepdog and the mountain behind; the cottage, the walls, one cow and his mother's apron, clouds and daisies all were white. Everything had become quite still, for a moment; it

19

seemed as though all movement froze, toy figures in a modelled background, like those sets in the town shops, or as though this was a painting done only in blue and white, black and grey. He had forgotten, his mother's headscarf, another cat, and the roof, were grey; so was the mist coming in, as he had turned, from the sea. You would have had to make the grass bright green though, he thought.

Of her six sons, all had gone except Miceal, who made scarce a living from his land, but was content with it.

Two with her, under the stones of the mountain, and Conal and Milo away in England on the farms, and the young Paudi, also in England, at anything at all.

Paudi was the wild one, never at anything for long, often on the road. He was back and forth over the Irish Sea like the colt breaking first into the one field then into another. Content with neither and with the feeling that he was missing something in the one he'd just left.

Paudi enjoyed his own voice and was argumentative though without having the wit or learning to construct or defend his views. He was dark and at first glance handsome, but when seen closer certain slips, like faults in rock, became visible. His face could change so that he no longer seemed good looking. His bright blue eyes would not be held, and had the same unbalanced shine of certain greyhounds. He was a devil with women, he liked to think, and was such a clever talker he could lead astray a Plato, both ending up by brilliantly speaking on subjects neither knew how they came to, and which meant nothing at all. Paudi was a magpie with language; he picked out bright phrases and glitter-laughter, he stole from literary nests. Such a voice naturally charms the ears off women and horses, and can lead a man away on a brilliant verbal jig which leaves him breathless at the finish, but no better off. Paudi was an Irish Orpheus, his voice his lute.

Miceal was dark too, as were most of the island men, with black hair as thick as a bullock's curling at his neck, and the pale, startling eyes of his mother. They had the same strange, unexpected quality as those of jackdaws and the silver-eyed merle sheepdog. Dark and light exchange. With the same impact as when a jet black horse turns not a brown eye to you, but a china stare.

Dark clothes, dark faces; the figures of the island men were dark, in a dark landscape. They stood quite still, like statues, in fields, at the sea's edge, on a headland. The tall dark standing stone would move and become a man. The women were in movement; sometimes a bright colour in a skirt or headscarf, which shouted in the rare sun. They would pause in their work to watch the stranger, with heavy stares like bullocks, but it was a pause only, and not the long looking, the communion of the men.

They were like statues placed here and there to watch the centuries stride past the island; their purpose now unknown, their design most ancient. The men stood and had forgotten why.

On bright days, from the furthest distance you could see clearly the white milk-can in a man's hand, or the tinny flash of fish on a string, so intensely luminous

21

the eye would bruise with colour. Light, that came in stealth with the cold dawn, needling and ferretting over the rocks and prominences, sending the shadows rabbitting for cover; light that triumphantly unrolled the colours of the island so that every field and bog and lake flew its flag of mustard yellows, violets and greens, printed with the blue of scabious, the red poppies and the white pennants of the bog cotton.

It flashed off the white cottages, which on Aranchilla seemed not to have been put together nor built at all, but put down by the hand, and pressed well in to the turf to firm them in.

Light transformed the lake to sapphire and the rivers to bronze, signalled among the quartz stones, ricochetted off walls. Cart wheels fizzed like comets, horses' shoes spun like sixpences; the light frothed and flickered and flung out the patched quilt of the island to the sun.

Everything steamed and shimmered as though a thousand lids were off the puddles and their stones nearly soft to the fork, and the roads writhed like cooking eels. On these days the sky full-sailed over Aranchilla, and the sea flung a rainbow at every headland.

And the people of the island, though watchful for the wind's dog that circles unseen to nip in when the jacket is off, would smile and bless the day.

They knew well how the grey storm, the wind dog's master, can rise in minutes out of the Atlantic, and snatch off all the colours, twist the heads from the flowers, clear the washing lines, anger the lake, jump on every beast's back and hammer his sides, and cut the smile from the sun's face with one swipe. It was therefore not often a man took off his coat for very long, and when he did, never left it far off.

The only one not caught out at all was the mountain,

who wound a cloud round his bald rock at the first spit, and accepted the inevitable.

This was the land that had made Miceal; made him of darkness and thought, from rocks and waters of endurance, of the quick light.

He went down to his aunt's croft to see what help she needed that day. His own hay was cut, Minna's yet to fall. Neighbours would come to both, and they would help them in turn.

The Kenny boys were in the yard, and Minna would have a load of sea-weed from them for her back patch, she thought. He climbed on to the trailer with young Sean, and the dogs jostled for places beside them.

The tractor banged along the dunes and one of the dogs fell off; Pat drove like a madman, and they roared at him to slow down a bit, ye mad whore.

At the yellow and blue tent, the fair girl and her friends were cooking something over their fire; a young man lay crucified in sleep on his back with a pink beach hat over his face. She looked up and seeing Miceal, waved. He got a dig from Sean.

As they turned down on to the strand they saw a dark girl walking towards the group of horses at the far end. Miceal remembered her, she had been one of those round the tent the first time he passed.

She won't get far with them, he thought. She'll get the arse kicked off her, boy, Pat shouted over one shoulder.

The horses' ears were set at her in audience, their eyes on her bulging as they do when a horse tries to look straight at something, and not trying it first with one and then the other.

She stood still. The white horse looked out to sea

uncertainly, then suddenly walked towards her.

Hearing the tractor she turned to look, and the thread snapped. The white horse wheeled away, then slowed and chose his way up the pebbles, followed slowly by the others. The dark girl picked up a stone and threw it high. Jesus, she's a mane like a horse too, said Sean.

Some people can do anything with horses. I'd like to get a holta that filly myself, boy, Pat whispered through his teeth.

Ah, shut up. Miceal forked up the first strands on to the trailer, but let his glance follow her over the fork. A pink father and his shrimp family appeared on the dunes, and the inevitable plastic ball bounced onto the beach in front of them, rolling to a disappointed stop, like a bore seeking a suitable victim in an empty bar.

The village had rubbed the dust from its thatched eyes by now. Carpets were hung out over bushes, cats escaped from the domestic turmoil, washing-lines dressed overall, and old backs creaked as their owners bent painfully to the ropes of tethered cows, humped and black, long-haired and anchored like currachs, chewing their ground-swell cud.

Mrs. Nolan brightly hung out her poor bird to take the air under the swinging 'Sea View'; Mrs. Nolan loved fresh air, and a gale usually blew through her house as a result, swelled and bellied through her open windows, and belched the back door open so that nothing ever shut properly. The bird had a mariner's list through constantly straining to keep his perch, and didn't dare turn away from the wind in case all his feathers blew off.

Garda John Mulloy, feeling under the Rhode Island for his special brown egg, found none, and told her plainly and distinctly she was a contrary old whore, felt again round her twiggy legs and was rewarded for his rudeness with an egg of a different colour.

Run the tap, woman, run the bloody tap, roaring into the kitchen with his hand stuck out like a frying pan on fire.

What in God's name is the matter, as Mrs. Mulloy ran, fearing he'd at least cut if off altogether. Shite woman, shite.

Philomena Mulloy, long used to insults, resigned herself for another of John's off-days and did as she was told, not realising that this time he made no more than a plain statement.

Mrs. Letitia Baggot, butcher, stirred late from a long and involved dream in which she had first neatly charted in the relevant cuts in marking ink upon her late husband's body, which had somehow obligingly laid itself out for this purpose on her marble slab, and, considering she had buried him eleven years at Christmas, he was miraculously fresh.

She had then cut him up easily and with not a hitch, and hung him, wrapped in bits of Xmas paper all over the shop ceiling, not so much to tempt the public to try him, but as a novel kind of interior decoration, a sort of fleshly mobile, for Mrs. Baggot prided herself on being 'contemprary' in all she did. Her house and shop, to this end, were painted a turgid lung-pink, the doors and windows a bright, arterial red.

Mrs. Baggot woke and her dream slithered lumpily out of her hand like an ox kidney, just as she was about to hang the legs, hooked by their Achilles tendons, on either side of the chimney. She had thought, with a chuckle, Sure, and won't oul Father Xmas be set back to find a real leg in each o' them oul' socks. No need to fill these, Mam, he'll say, I see they're full already, Heh, heh, hay hay and even in her dream Mrs. Baggot was aware she'd nearly pissed herself. Three little wizened pieces left, the late Mr. Baggot had never exercised these as he should, and the eyeballs. She was not sure how to dispose of these. Even in a dream there's some decency. But even in a dream there was always the cat.

♘

Mrs. Baggot, if the theory is correct that ancient strains crop up unexpectedly, was a direct descendant of Pithecanthropus. That her son Leonard was so good looking remained a genetic mystery, since the departed Mr. Baggot was not handsome either, and though neither blind nor drunk as might be supposed when he bedded with his simian lady, soon solved the problem by becoming both together all the time, and never went near her again until prematurely swept into his coffin by a tide of ale and a bullocking consumption.

To Mrs. Baggot's way of thinking, he had suffered a most satisfactory haemorrhage. All over the new bathroom decorated by herself with the same tiles she had used in the slaughter house.

Just like a pig he was.

Everywhere. Even up to the ceiling. Just like a pig, God rest his soul.

♞

Leonard Baggot, who did the actual killing much to his mother's disappointment, dreamed of girls. Girls of all kinds and all colours.

26

Each one he led tenderly stark naked to a flowery cave/bower/altar, said I will in a loud voice to Father Muldoon, and still tenderly, placed the humane-killer between their eyes.

The black girls, having, he'd read somewhere, thicker skulls, he shot near the ears, like horned sheep.

A pattering like rain, and a string of meagre little asses, punctuating every pointed step with a nod as though they'd mentioned the Holy name with every hoof, wound through the village on their way to the strand.

There they would stand, or sometimes lie if trade eased, all day in any weather, like a convention of small grey philosophers. Youths whacked and shouted at them, and cowboyed up and down in front of the girls, children vented their parent's spleen on their bushy ribs; only the girls were sometimes nice to them.

They had Diarmuid, Balor, Cuchulain, Grainne and other unsuitable mythological titles engraved on their brow-bands. Their owner, Manny O'Hehir, a simple being who had once loved Eileen O'Shaughnessy so deeply that it had turned his head, was called, not unkindly, Creeping Jesus. Not only because he was slightly bearded, and this due to no biblical aspirations but to lack of a good razor and will power, but because he always rode the last and smallest ass in the un-ruffled, unhurrying little bunch. He took seven league strides to each of her four tittups, his feet pedalling on the road each side of her.

The last ass was his favourite.

Her name was Eileen.

John Joseph Feeney, alias Smirky, was scratching and yawning in the Select Bar, blinking and snuffling like a badger fresh from hibernation. John Joseph seldom spoke. When he did, he threw his spare words on to the tables of his customers as he threw them their drinks and their change. Tourists chatted brightly to him at first, but soon gave up, nonplussed.

Remarks addressed to him half an hour previously would be suddenly answered in another room, or out in the yard, almost never to those who had spoken to him.

In the partitioned shop of his establishment, a cabbage would be lifted, examined as though of some rare and precious material and told Aye, yeh can get a boat for the day from oul Clancy Perkins. To a child's bucket and spade set, He lives but a hen's race down the road from here, and a jar of peppermints, critically examined as though they were vital to research heard, The house has Stella Maris written up, yeh cannot miss it.

He smiled fondly at a packet of hairnets. Aye, a bad day, sure enough, But 'twill rise up later, one of his cows was glad to hear.

Suddenly coming up behind a group of visitors he would put an arm round them, saying nothing, but after examining each face carefully, as though looking for flaws in a diamond, he would smile most amiably into each pair of astonished eyes.

Over the years his words grew less, and his smiling examinations more pronounced.

Keys, bananas, gratings over drains, tooth brushes, his toenails, young carrots though not old ones, scissors, collars on dogs, walls; all were appraised and re-examined with the same appreciation that God must have warmly felt on the seventh day.

No-one ever saw him different; it was always old

Smirky, a character mind you, but a decent man.

No-one ever saw him when he went into his locked shed where, at the back of the crates and piled bottles, he carefully pulled the heads off an endless, standing order of mauve jelly-babies. The other colours were left for the shop. Only the mauve ones lost their suggary smiles as Smirky's grew wider.

There were four Feeney brothers, and only Smirky was left on Aranchilla. Peter, known as Re-Peter Feeney because of his habit of repeating everything he said, came over from England once a year to drive the rest of Smirky's customers, already somewhat startled by Smirky, completely out of the Select Bar. He was fat, with pale ginger hair, and a white face which sweated permanently like lard. His pink neck bulged out from under his ears which were also fringed with ginger. He never appeared to open his small puffy eyes at all. He bore down on those seated outside on fine days, squinting down on them through piggish ginger eyelashes and giving them the uncomfortable feeling they were trapped in a stye with a Tamworth boar. As he also possessed an unfortunate impediment to his speech, together with lips like a mullet, his conversations were like those of a pig talking through mouthfulls of swill. His R's were mouthed and chased like the odd potato at the trough bottom, and he swallowed the end of each sentence with a shake of his chops. Small children were completely fascinated by him, particularly when he oinked with laughter. He veered from Manchester to Irish like a bi-lingual barometer. Arr joost coom buck from Bunchester. Bunchester. Aye, Bunchester. T'is a fine city, a fine city, aye, a very fine city. D'ye know it, d'ye know it at all? Will it be yeh first visit, is it yeh first visit, have yeh not been here before? Yeh have not, I could see yeh have not.

I have milk, I shall have milk this night for yeh baby, aye the baby. It will cost yeh nothing, I charge nothing. Terrible fond of the childer, a dote for the childer, Aye.

Never had any childer meself, none meself. Never married, yeh know. Never married. No, never married. Though I could, many times, many's the time . . . oink. Aye, indeed.

No, I never married and I loves the childer. Yup. Yeh've a lovely woman there, sir, a lovely woman. Yes indeed. A lovely woman. Such hair, yeh know; like the Chinese. Many Chinese yeh know in Bunchester. Lovely people the Chinese. Yup.

Of the other two Feeney brothers, one came home every two years, the other every three, and all went straight to milk the cows as though they'd only been to market and got held up on the road back for a few years.

There was no need for them to have milked the cows at all, Smirky was already there, but they all did on returning to Aranchilla, the two from England, and the one from America. Strangely the cows never missed one lapse of attention, however thick the heads the next morning, and no Feeney ever missed his turn, or rusted with lack of use.

Re-Peter from Manchester, Malachy from Birmingham, Paddy from Brooklyn, all homed straight to the byre, and no lovers, after a long parting, fell into each others' arms half as fondly as the sixteen black tits fell into the warmly receptive Feeney fingers.

The first bus of the day, which was also the last bus on its way back, encircled the island for the convenience of those tourists without transport, and was a means for everyone on Aranchilla to have at least one weekly opportunity to see what everyone else was doing.

Driver Casey, a great reader and reciter of the classic Irish sagas and legends, and a firm believer in his own descent from Cuchulain himself, would climb up into his chariot and set the Raven and the Grey alight. The inhabitants and the tourists could be easily distinguished; those still in their seats were inhabitants, those on the floor tourists. The outward conductor Flaming James Kelly, red-topped as a furze fire, beat open and kicked shut the door for each passenger with an energy so frenzied, traumatic tourists would think either the President himself was about to enter, or that the large hairy dog that had climbed in at the previous village had now gone beserk and must be got out at all costs.

The homeward conductor, an Irish survival from the same ancient tap-root as Mrs. Baggot, was enormous and melancholy. He had black thickets where most have eye-brows, brow ridges like Dordogne cliffs, and great jaws that revolved whether he spoke or not. He bent to the violence of the bus with sagging knees which made his arms seem longer than they were, and his hands, awkward as stranded octopuses, were so large they had difficulty holding anything as flimsy as a ticket. Dim, ponderous Thomas Ryan resembled the least bright ape which never achieves the grape at the end of the experiment.

He bent over each passenger in turn and sadly enquired How is ut, to which he received various responses according to whether the one addressed thought it was a fine day, thought it was a lousy day, had corns, had shopped cunningly, had sold badly at market, was

31

going to or from a wake, had piles.

Possibly due to the perpetual damp there were many sufferers from this complaint. They were another easily recognisable faction in the bus's hierarchy. They were the ones who never quite sat down; who, gripping the rails, like good jockeys rose well at every jump.

Whether fanfared in or out by Flaming James Kelly, or solicituously gloomed over by Thomas Ryan, the chariot was always curbed in half-way. Woaa, lads, Woa-hoa at Mulrany's Bar for the ladies to look at the scenery. Just a wee bit down the road, Mam, a lofley view.

And the ladies, when they got there, if tourists, were surprised at the lack of any scenery at all except several large bushes, but thankful for Cuchulain's tact and foresight. And the men thundered gladly into Mulrany's for a quick jar that, with luck, might last the hour if all went well, and none of the ladies was a sprinter or consumed with that distressing sense of haste so prevalent amongst the foreigners.

On leaving, Mr. Casey would take the reins from his imaginary attendant struggling to hold back the impetuous pair, and holding them high so that they wouldn't get entangled round the bonnet, would leap lightly into the chariot, and signal to the now suspended lad to let them go. Down would come the rearing heads of the Raven and the Grey, and the chariot would jerk forward. The masterly handling of the reins was observed by the waiting complement, but was put down as a stiff arm due to the bad roads.

The deafening crash of branches, when the swerving bus appeared to scratch an itchy flank, was also accepted as all part of the journey. No-one noticed, as Mr. Casey did through his rear mirror, the legless body of Connaught's finest champion lying in the ditch, literally cut

32

down in his prime by masterly use of the sickles on the hub-caps.

The Long Man Brannigan, nearly seven feet of him, walked back with his peculiar long stride from the harbour quay, his black currach humped and stranded like a small black whale. He was a great fisherman, on all waters; on the lakes and rivers, or at sea.

He seemed to be always looking out, distantly, over water, unable to focus on the lesser things of the land. So tall, he looked at you with the pale, downward stare of a bittern. He walked with his body stiffly upright, his eyes unfocused, his legs wading him on with great pushing strides, as though he was taking on the Atlantic. He was deaf and dumb. No one knew his age, and very few remembered when he was neither deaf nor dumb at all, and ready to marry Bridie McDonagh, of a mainland village round the next bay.

Bridie had had other ideas though, and hadn't considered telling them to an island man. She married Tommy Quinn, all teeth and money, with two handsome shops in the two biggest towns in the County Louth, and no knowledge at all of boats or of the sea.

The Long Man had given them their wedding gift, though he said nothing to them, nor would ever speak again.

He stepped up to the bride at her reception in the grand mainland hotel and gave her a small white box such as shoes are packed in. When Bridie opened it, a little uncomfortable with the Long Man standing there staring at her, saying nothing, in his best black clothes, there inside lay a beautiful fair haired doll, dressed like herself in a white wedding gown.

They could all see the Long Man was not in his right mind. Tommy Quinn insisted the doll be given back or thrown away. Even his suburban heart felt something was wrong, that ill luck was present.

The Long Man took the box away with him, all the way home to the island, to the back of his small white house, where he buried the doll in her white box and went out to sea.

The only arms that welcomed him now were the cold stone arms of the harbour when he returned out of the net of darkness night threw over the sea.

๑

Mrs. Have-Patience Geraghty prepared to welcome her annual visitors to the typical island cottage, all conveniences, in beautiful surroundings, very reasonable. The saturated travellers found themselves, after hours of driving through blinding rain and a succession of forbidding crags and endless bogs, with the occasional hunched and sodden ass to add to their hazards on the road, confronted by a small bearded woman with Pekinese eyes and one tooth. These together with a grip like a gin, was Mrs. Geraghty, who steamed out with the cabbage to greet them and conduct them to the typical island home. Mr. Geraghty was packed out of the back door at the sound of their car, as bottles are swept away, or the remains of dinner.

He was fortunate not to have been shut into a cupboard or covered with the table cloth where he sat, but Mrs. Geraghty was a great believer in appearances, and Willie, being the most contrary wretch a poor woman ever had to put up with, would be sure either to fall out of the cupboard together with its entire contents, or sneeze and blow off his tablecloth, and she'd have a tiresome half-hour trying to explain him away. Mr. Geraghty never complained. He locked the back door behind him, his wife being afraid of a mass descent of all the Dublin gangs on her living room if the place was left unguarded for a moment, and sat among the hens smoking his pipe and awaiting his recall to the stringy bosom of his family.

Mrs. Geraghty, flashing her eyes like well-aimed marbles up to the Almighty, to whom she unceasingly called upon to act as her witness and legal advisor, conducted her guests up a steep track which also appeared to be a small river's bed, and the typical island home could be seen in the distance, in its beautiful surroundings of bog.

I said to meself when yeh had not arrived, I said we must have Patience, mam. We must always have Patience. They too must have Patience, I said mam, the poor souls out there on the road, and I must have Patience too, waiting for yeh to arrive.

The conveniences were exhibited; electricity was certainly there, borne crackling over the bog on great galloping supports as though something from another planet was invading the island in steel leaps. Running water Mam, there's running water for yeh. All off the mountain. None purer. It cannot go stale on yeh when it's running.

It ran from the bottom of a curious cement structure, which resembled a shrine without its statue.

By now, unless Americans, who were steadfastly enchanted by the cuteness of it all, all so *maidly* primitive, the distraught visitors would be shown their last convenience; its door wedged with a white quartz stone. So roughly constructed, so small and so far away from its parent residence, it looked like the retreat of a hermit, who was not only a midget, but judging from

35

his tottering cell, none too clever with his hands neither.

Rule number wan. Mrs. Geraghty ticked off her commandments on a badgery paw. Yeh pays for the gas. Rule number two, I supply the turr-uf. Rule number three, I do the toilet, I always do the toilet, yeh've no need to give it another thought.

Payment Mam? I am not worried. Just when yeh please. We must all have Patience, and it will all come right at the very end I always found Mam. Life is terrible queer Mam, but I always say, we must have Patience at all times. Money is not everything Mam, as heaven is my witness it is not.

The Legal Adviser received another nudge, and her hand fastened on her visitors' like a pike's jaws.

Cead Mile Failte, that's what we all say here Mam. A hundred thousand welcomes, and God give yeh the powerful weather.

And Mrs. Geraghty withdrew to her own typical island home, pulling pleasantly at her whiskered chin, feeling the crisp lettuce money in her pocket and muttering Cead Mile Failte to herself. Willie Geraghty heard her unlock the front door with her own key, and knocked out his pipe expectantly.

Mrs. Geraghty called out to her husband, now bent waiting key ready, at the back door Yeh can come in now, yeh big ape.

Mr. Geraghty edged uneasily into his only chair, smelling sourly of chickens, disappointment and neglect.

A hare watched them through the window from where he sat on the top of their wall, his ears scissoring, his nose analysing the aromatic peculiarities left behind by Mr. Geraghty, who had, like a billy goat, contributed a certain lurking pungency to the surroundings.

Father Connolly spent his summers with Father Muldoon, helping with Masses when the island was flooded with the extra souls. He had come to Aranchilla since a young man, first on his holidays as he liked the place, then to stay at the parish house as part of his work. He was greatly loved by the islanders for his gentleness and courtesy. He spoke of charity, and hope and sweetness, and heard their confessions with a tolerance and understanding far removed from the blasting operations of the black-browed Father Muldoon. Father Connolly was never professedly horrified by his fellow men, seldom condemnatory, and never, despite the perversness and treachery in the world, without the deepest faith in the triumph of good in Man and the conviction of his ultimate perfection. Whereas Father Muldoon saw everybody from birth as deeply black with original sins as his own black Mayo bogs, excavating for them in his flock with great hewing sermons and charges of damnation.

Father Connolly found God everywhere; in daisies and windbells, in a nest of eggs, in a coloured pebble, expectedly and unexpectedly, and in the ordered worlds of beasts.

He believed in the former, lost ability of man to live in complete harmony with his fellow creatures, to be as serene in his surroundings as a tree or a bird, as naturally part of his ecology as the mineral in the rock. Composed of stars and oceans, jewels and clay, divided though undivided, he saw man, too, had had as formal a pattern to his living as the swan that only takes another swan to himself, as formal as the ritual bee. If only, thought Father Connolly, the unimaginable gift of his intellect could have shown him himself as a whole, of God become aware, of the ineffable architect who created the cathedral of his form, and the vaulted chambers of his spirit. Father Connolly walked slowly down the strand, thinking of the grains of human life, of what man was before the changing fragments of his antique design left the first cooling crucible.

A creature of sublime destruction and cataclysmic creation, of silence and music, nebulae and spiral vortices, wheeling through spectrums and alchemies. Still unknown to himself.

Father Connolly, kneeling like a hound, grieved a sudden, desperate prayer to the sky. O God. Help us. *Help us.*

He was filled with an unutterable sadness. He turned back feeling cold, and stood for a moment as though blind. A dead ray, shredded and fibred as a torn kite, smiled up from its corruption. Father Connolly thought only the frame will be left soon, then only the bony rasp of its smile remain.

He felt suddenly happier.

A smelly, tattered, obscene object, even its sex a triangular parody of Man's. Yet how right, he thought, that it should wear the double mask of comedy in its tragedy.

🐎

Philomena Mulloy watched her man John wheel out his bicycle. He slammed the gate of her heart. A simple woman, she felt sometimes there was a side to her husband she knew nothing about. She was right. Even as a girl, she had suffered from a nervous, cringing disposition, the kind of face which asked to be slapped despite piteous appeals to the contrary. She had the unhappy knack of always saying and doing the exasperatingly wrong things. She brought disasters to fruition. John Mulloy now found her unbearable, and told her

38

so as often as he could. He had only married her for the marvellous upholstery she had carried as a girl beneath her unskillfully home knitted jumpers.

For Garda Mulloy, the female bosom contained everything essential to Man's fullest ideals of pleasure and beauty.

He saw breasts everywhere, on mountains, in tea cups, ink-wells, hats with pom-poms, fires, tea-cosies, clouds, electric light switches, cows, jelly moulds, loaves of bread, in dreams and the Kremlin. He examined every female visitor as openly as the judge at a class for Frisian heifers. He was saddened by drooping or fallen ones, overjoyed with those that prodded and bounced. He was an expert on shapes and kinds, from Masai to Bali, from the Stone Age to Rubens, Goya and Port Said, and he dreamed of highly international beauty contests judged by feel only, himself the sole adjudicator.

Poor Philomena had long since flattened into anonymity and lost her only attraction for John, who found anyway he could not perform at the length and with the subleties he craved for under that damned picture of Our Lord she had to have wincing down on the nuptial bed.

It completely put him off, with one hand raised as though in pious horror at what was in his mind, and the other coyly squeezing the bleeding heart between ladylike finger and thumb, as you hold out a dead rat.

And Thou Shalt Not in Gothic lettering on every pulsating drop. And as if that wasn't enough, a blasted framed text at eye level, with the same heart, though this time with improbable flames coming out of its top, like an old-fashioned Bolshevik grenade, and Cease! Thy Kingdom Come.

To add to her husband's displeasure, Philomena

could not control a distressing affliction; she farted continuously. Everything she did was to a concerto of extraordinary variety and virtuousity. Her day began beside the irate John, with the effort of rising to a rapid small-arms fire, and ended beside him with a despairing Last Post, as through a rubber trumpet.

House work was accomplished to shrill whistlings, a sneeze brought a startling choked pop. Periods of rest, with her feet up and her tea beside her was a comforting relaxation of long, emptying balloons.

The stairs she truly dreaded. Up or down, they caused her to sound off like a fast trotting horse.

She tried hard to stifle them when John was around, and sand-bagged her worst with agonised control. And suffered doubly as a result, not only from his unkind remarks but from her pent-up explosions.

The Garda Mulloy, out of uniform, meanwhile greeted every startled female visitor with a quick assessment of their potential or visible assets. That's a nice pattern you're wearing, Mam. The Aran is the best of all for showing yeh all to the best advantage. Oh, grand, it is.

Usually the astonished lady was too amazed to protest, and not sure whether she was hearing properly. Perhaps he meant something else; you couldn't tell half the time what these extraordinary islanders were talking about. John Mulloy never fully understood the annoyance he seemed to cause. They should have been pleased at his compliments. Sure, women were a queer tribe altogether. If they hadn't such a powerful set of lollopers on the front of them what the hell would we want to be talking with them at all.

It was the holiday season, after all; the time for enjoyment and bikinis and he'd read all the English girls were good for anything, and not stuck up at all.

He thought angrily of all the varied and delightfully

40

subtle things he could do to them all, at which even the foreigners could only guess and gasp, and told the Long Man Brannigan as he loped by. I didn't come up the river on the first fecking bubble, yeh know.

To which he received no answer, but the long double bore stare of a heron eyeing an eel.

And the tinkers, on the edges of the island, always on the edges of the lands and the settled society, prepared to move on. The young boys were ordered out of the lake where they had been bathing, their skinny white bodies silvery as sand eels. The girls fanned out to bring in the band of wandering asses and their foals. The splashed horses were harnessed up, wraps, blankets and tarpaulins hauled off bushes and shafts and flung up into the orange and yellow and blue carts, the women wound their shawls, hitched up skirts and babies, and climbed into the carts. Hysterical dogs ran under all feet, there were shouts, whinnies, brayings, barks and children's laughter.

Then the horses' feet sparking on the road and the children strung out, walking, driving the asses in front of them.

The Dorans were off for the ferry over to the mainland, none of them bothered by the stares and the withdrawings of their fellow travellers on board, fearful of their cars touching the high-wheeled carts, the shaggy heads of the horses resting against their rear windows.

A man in a white, comic fringed hat followed on a bicycle, a small dog attacking the tyres. Far behind, a pair of young donkeys, roped together, squeaked and bucked beneath the weight of the last Doran, who lay across them both as comfortably and unperturbed as

though slung in a hammock. Through bushes, down
hollows, up banks, over the sand dunes, braying and
kicking, the hilarious trio sped in incompatible disorder. Where they had camped under a high bank, the
big black and white gulls scuttled and quarrelled among
the tins and rags and the warm ashes of their fire.

Miceal and the Kelly boys worked all day at the heavy
kelp. They watched the girls from the blue and yellow
tent come down to the strand and walk away to the
curve of the bay where they swam. Of the three boys
with them, from the small khaki tent beside theirs, two
ran around with a ball and hackneyed about the beach,
like bloody eejits as Pat said, and the dark one sat
alone on the dunes writing rapidly. His face was con-
centrated and blank to the shouts of the others.

Miceal could see his cows away under the cliff at the
far end of the strand, a deceiving nearness to them
when it was all of two miles to where they grazed. The
curve of the sands and the winding river in between
slid you a mile back before you knew it, as the tourists
found when they set off for the black cliffs as just a
step away, and wondered when the hell they were going
to get there, if at all, and if it wasn't all a mirage. He
decided to make this the last load, then fetch home his
cows.

'Tis only the girls being there, Mick.

Go on, yeh've left the beasts to look after themselves
often enough.

The two boys joined Miceal as he turned down the
strand, his dog weary with the heat, low-brushed as a
fox.

That's heavy stuff, isn't it. Seeing you working hard
all day made us feel guilty.

Ah, there's no need when you're on your holidays, now.

Didn't know you'd tractors in this place.

Yesterday there was a shuttle-service of donkeys staggering up the beach with loads of the stuff all over them.

Where do you come from?

Miceal showed them the white disc of the cabin high above the lake.

I have to fetch the beasts home for the night's milking, they're slow to come when the day's fine at all.

We'll walk on a bit with you then.

I'm Henry, by the way, Henry Hughes.

This is Stew, he's from Canada, Stewart McKenzie.

The tall fair lad smiled behind thick glasses, shook Miceal's hand hard. Pleased to know you.

Henry nodded back at the dunes. That black object up there is the mad one among us, Ran. He's the poet. We're all a bit mad I suppose, but he's definitely nothing else.

Yeh'll be on yeh're holidays then.

Stew is, so'm I, and so are two of the girls. The other two are more or less permanently given to them. We seek enlightenment and women in far places, my friend.

Miceal did not understand them completely and felt awkward.

That's a nice dog you've got there. What's his name? And your's too, we didn't ask you. I'm sorry.

Miceal. He pronounced it in Irish.

That's Michael, isn't it? Aye, we most of us have the Gaelic here, a great number of teachers and students come each summer to speak it. The dog has no name. We don't go in much for naming beasts here. I think the Ma called him Bruno one time.

They fitted their steps into his rhythm. Stew took off his pink straw hat and waved it to the girls. They were sitting under the high ridge of pebbles rising steeply off the sands up to the dunes behind. The dark one waved an orange towel back.

The fair girl was combing her long silky hair, now stiff from the sea.

Stew knelt dramatically, his arms out.

Ah Rumpelstiltskin, let down thy hair. That I may climb up it and perchance up thee as well. Henry looked at Miceal, dark and composed, waiting. Don't worry Mike. You'll get used to us. We're not really dangerous except at feeding time.

It wasn't Rumpelstiltskin. Wasn't he the one with the long whiskers who fell asleep for a hundred years. Clot, that was Rip Van Winkle. Oh yes, so it was. But I'm sure it was Rumpelstiltskin. Funny how annoying it is — Dee-dee-dee, dah-dah-dah, let down thy hair. Sister Anne, Sister Anne. No, I'm wrong again. She looked out of a window or a mirror or something.

And Time and the World are ever in flight. The dark-headed one stood above them on the dunes. Oh, hello Ran. Out of your Celtic twilight, lad, and down to these yellow sands. Let's foot it feetly back, my swan maidens, and start the supper.

This is Miceal. Mee-hawl, Irish for Mike. Look, what about coming to supper with us tonight. Will you? We'd all be delighted. How long does it take to collect the cows and get down here again? Do you walk, or have you a bike?

I would be down around eight if that will not be too late for you. 'Tis a long toil up there and the cows slow. Aye, I would say eight.

OK with us.

Ran jumped down the pebbles to them. He was tall

44

and thin, with shaggy black hair and a black circle of narrow beard.

Randall Hennessy, so it is, so it is. He's Irish too. Ran, meet Mike. He bowed. How are the squitters, lad. He's had them since we've been here, something he's eaten I suppose or the water. Flies up and down to the bushes like a greyhound.

O What can ail thee Knight At Arms, alone and palely loitering, what ails thee, what ails thee, Lord Randall my son?

Ah, stuff it said the beard bleakly.

Yeh sound from Dublin, Miceal asked.

I am, though I go there as little as possible.

They wandered on past the girls. Hurry up you women and get dressed. We're starving. Let's sit and wait for your cows to catch up, Mike. They're coming along slowly on their own, look.

For a while, then.

They handed cigarettes, insisted Miceal had one, leaning back against the pebbles. Miceal sat forward, his hands knotted between his knees. The collie came round to his side and lay down, tense, waiting for his next move.

What d'yeh do, back home?

Henry shaded his eyes. I'm at medical college, dear lad. I feel the urge to take suffering humanity to my little hairy bosom, and cure its afflictions with noble dedication. At least I think I do.

Come unto me, ye nadgered.

Stew here is On Vacation as he calls it.

I'm over to see a bit of Ireland, Mike. Some of my ancestors came from Tipperary. They were Purcells. Do you know of them at all?

No, I've not heard that name, though round here names are not the same as in other parts, I'm told.

I'm at University, doing various things. Medieval History, and ... He glanced at Miceal. Poor sod he thought, hasn't a clue what we're on about. He did not want to appear rude. Lots of useless things he said. We're a sunny open lot with sunny open faces, Mike. At the threshold of our young lives. God I'm hungry. Hey, Britt, what's for supper, hon?

The girls were very brown, Miceal thought, not looking directly. You could tell the Irish among the visitors by their whiteness. Sun like these past few days was rare on Aranchilla. The fair girl smiled at him. Hello. I've seen you about quite a lot.

He lives up there, miles up the mountain. Henry thumbed lazily.

Her hair is nearly white, Miceal thought. It was as pretty as a child's, and she looked like a tall child, with a sweetness about her, and she was completely natural.

She'd had on one of those bikinis, a pink one, and had slipped a white dress over it as they talked. He'd not noticed. He had felt awkward, not able to look directly at their brown bodies in the bright swim suits.

That's Britt, our cook, She's Swedish.

Well, they all cook, but somehow we think of Britt as the Mamma Mia who brakes all our bread. And Letty, she's the middle one there. A nice girl, but she doesn't let anyone. Henry avoided the flail of seaweed. Letty Humphries, from Cornwall. That's in England, just. They're all Celts there too, like you and Ran. A real Cornish pasty, aren't you love, stuffed into that two piece. Come over here a minute and I'll pop you in my little oven and do you to a turn, anyway do you to a turn.

He fled up the beach as Letty erupted.

She was a short, stolid girl with spiky brown hair

46

and a good-humoured face. I saw you with that horse this morning.

Miceal looked up into the long brown eyes of the dark girl. Her black hair fell down her back very straight and shining wet still, like a seal's coat. She wore a long red skirt, and a red brassiere.

He felt uncomfortable over it, though a bikini top was far less he thought. You stupid gombeen. Her flowered swimsuit dried on the pebbles.

Yes, she's our dark horse. Ran put an arm around her. She ducked from under it. Almost literally, Mike.

Miceal said: You won't get far with that grey. He's been let away for years now.

Your tractor frightened him. He'll come again.

She looked at him, sideways, her long brown eyes showing the whites very clearly in the brown face.

He thought she looks at you like one too.

I must away now, he said.

Henry came back with Letty. She was laughing, swinging a towel. He kicked a stone beside her, now serious, his eyes aloof. Britt, Mike's coming to supper. OK with you? Oh yes. Please come Mike. We're having a stew, so come when you can. It won't spoil.

The collie's hard eyes flickered from face to face, his nose veering, his tail shivering.

I'll see you then. Thank you. All the best now.

Miceal felt like a thunderstorm, crashing over the pebbles in his thick boots, as thick and black and heavy as a bloody bullock he thought. The collie sped in front of him searching with head high for sight of the cows.

They were just over the ridge and nearly up with him, the square black bodies ambling slowly, tails and heads swinging at the flies. They stumbled and slid over the pebbles down on to the sand, where they could cross the river at the shallows fanning out into the sea.

The others were some way ahead, the dark girl a distance behind, washing her towel and swimsuit in the fresh water.

A sound like a rush of coins made her look up. The band of horses was coming down on to the sands in front of her. The grey stopped to drink, his white reflection shaking around him. The rest wandered on, nosing and lipping among the seaweed.

Stew looked around. Jeez, they're terrific, horses sure look good by the sea. The white horse raised his head, water running from his working mouth, then slowly followed the others.

The cows rolled their stares at Selene, breathing at her suspiciously as they waded past, blowing huffs and streamers at her sandals left at the other side. She wrung out the clothes and waited for Miceal.

A crashing of stones and a strange roar made them turn together, and the cows scattered as another horse leaped down on to the beach, stretching over the wet sand and flashing his outlandish colours like the shrill jay.

Hey, he's a strange one, I've not seen him before. Holy Saints will yeh look at him go. Miceal was shouting.

The horse wore down on the startled band which had fled from his first burst, and who now faced him with heads stiff and high. The grey trotted back uncertainly and stopped, his tail over his back.

The stranger propped to a stand, spurting up the sand like the burrowing flounder. He shook his head, weaving it like a snake, his neck low, crouching at the ground like a leopard. His mane rippled like the frill of a sea-serpent.

The brown girl touched Miceal.

Oh isn't he beautiful, he's the most beautiful horse I've ever seen, he looks as though he's been carved out of different kinds of marble or precious stones.

I've not seen one like him before.

Miceal saw the others were watching as well. The tinkers have them sometimes, I'm told. They call them a mizzen-star.

The horse now had his head up, staring full and hard at the nodding grey.

He was curiously marked, veined pinks and reds marbled all over him, his eyes ringed with white like onyx, white streaks stormed up his back and black splashes threw a squalling pattern which seemed to change and fly with his movements.

The effect was bizarre, almost disturbing. As though he had exploded into life, like Pegasus from the Gorgon's head, born in a star-burst, or thrown up by the sea in a black squall.

A mizzen-star. What a marvellous name. The girl's face held a brightness, like someone near tears. He is a horse of the sea and the stars and the earth. He is universal Horse she said.

Miceal looked down at her. You surely love horses. He smiled. They didn't give me your name. Would I be right now in thinking you'll not be English.

I am Greek. She watched the horses intently, as though she directed them, knew what each would do. As though she was under the marbled hide on the sea's edge.

You wouldn't know my name, Miceal. You have

nothing like it over here, and it's not heard in Greece now, either. I am called Selene.

Selene. And if I'm not away now I'll not be back this night. The cows had taken themselves up the dunes and were padding quietly across the flat stretch of turf to the road home. The collie sat looking down at Miceal and back at the cows.

He followed them, turning now and again to watch the theatre of horses on the great curve of the bay. The white-headed collie fitted to his heels like a remnant of his own shadow. The red skirt of the dark girl, Selene, shone like the pimpernel against the black cliffs behind her.

The white horse had dropped his tail, there was a softening to his outline, a slackening of tension. He looked out over the sea, then back at the other horses, unthreading the spell which had held them in a checkmate of immobility.

The splashed horse stamped a foreleg, swung his head and snapped round at his side. He lanced himself into a quick jerking canter, squealing and snorting between curious short trilling barks. He snaked his head, bit the air, nipped his speckled chest. His striped mane flashed with each bound, and his tail, curved up over his short strong back, flew its pennants of hair like a pirate ship its colours.

The spots and splashes all over him mingled and re-formed with his movements, as though someone was painting him into life's startling design, writing him into the eye.

On each leg a flurry of black and white markings chased down to the hoofs, and a hail of white spattered his neck and forequarters. Black shoals of spots gathered and dived over the curve of his rump like a pouring of fish.

50

Like erased hieroglyphics, the colours scratched and ran together over the tomb of his big head, and Selene saw with amazement that one eye was pale brown, the other a cold blue.

You could hardly believe that he was real, that he was not carved from marble and amethyst, agate and onyx, the eyes set with a topaz and a moonstone, or his colours fired on him with an antique design of water and stars. Stick on the streamers of the windy cirrus, the horse-tails of the sky, and set your fanfare horse on fire.

There we go again, thought Selene ruefully.

Oh, you lovely, fantastic horse. His challenge was not answered. The grey turned for the dunes and plunged for the open heath behind, his company scattering behind him. Some followed him, the slower ones lessening speed and floundering as the spotted horse ground into them.

Aye, no gelding would stand against that one. Miceal tapped on his hot cows. That was an entire alright. Wonder did he throw his likeness on his stock. There'd be a great mixture on the island now, a grand race of mizzen-stars. He thought of his invitation to supper and prodded on the cows again. The collie ran in immediately to nip the heels of the last one, flashing a look into Miceal's face for approval.

On the track past the lake Miceal heard an outburst of whinnying and saw the horses had stopped running. The mizzen-star was squealing and striking at a mare. The grey was now alone, grazing by the bushes. They touched noses, triggering an explosion of squeals. Forelegs stamped and struck, tails lashing like angry cats. To each the stallion greeted, introduced, commanded and won.

At the croft Miceal looked down on the heath, gold

in the evening sunlight. All the horses grazed quietly now. A pencil of smoke was rising near the blue and yellow dot. He was suddenly hungry and remembered he must call in at the Minna's and tell her not to await supper for him. Please God she'd not take it against herself, women were grieveously given to taking offence where none was intended. The cows stopped by the door of the cabin, waiting for him to bring out the bucket and milk them where they stood like black wedges between the sunlight and the evening.

Garda John Mulloy was on his way home, on his last lap up to his house by the deserted tarred walls of the old harbour.

Thank the Lord Jesus for that, thought John, as he looked both ways and the Guinness fairly rattling to get out.

He pissed gratefully over the centre-bar of his bicycle, absently drawing a map of Europe on the blackboard surface. Too generous with his initial supply, he flooded Italy and crossed out Russia with a satisfying slash. The last few shaken drops flicked in the Aegean Islands most artistically, he thought.

Garda Mulloy varied his repertoire according to mood or the surface he had to work on. It was surprising what the oul' tool and bit of imagination could achieve, length of supply being the only problem.

The commotion among the horses had brought out the villagers to watch.

John thought this time the bastards must go. Find

who owns who, and get the lot impounded. Get them paying and they'll not be too quick about letting the damn things out again in a hurry. A danger to everyone, it was time the island was rid of them all. Rounded up and out of the way altogether, that queer yoke as well, wherever he'd sprung from. Roaring away like a bloody lion and no sight for the ladies.

All of them away, until there wasn't a beast on Aranchilla that wasn't hobbled in its owner's fields or at work as it should be. He'd like to beat the head off every damn one of them.

The whole of the island lay beneath Miceal as he drove the cows up to the small walled field on the mountain's edge for the night. The fowl would go in on their own at dusk. The white-headed collie he chained by the door as usual.

Minna was, as he expected, both avidly curious but critical of his new companions and full of warnings as to their undoubted immoral outlook and influence on himself.

Yeh'r worse than the good Father and that's little enough to recommend yeh.

The island was luminous with the blue on gold of the late evening. At morning both the colours merged intensely into a breathing, living white light, an unearthly quality of light that lay on and came out of the glittering island as though it was a diamond cut from the bedrock sea by the sun.

Now the white strand lay with the play of day over, an interval of light rather than time heralding the imperceptible change to the second act of night.

The golden haze of sunlight, the day's scents of sea

and heather as heavy on the senses as the flight of a drunken bee, were sharpening and cooling into a gentle blue soon to lengthen into purple and spire the shadows into nightfall.

Sounds were few, the haze absorbing them. The sea oiled and fingered the sands, floating away the untroubled weed, disturbing no shell with its quietness.

Selene sat alone on the sands, her chin on her knees. Britt was cooking, Letty washing her hair, and the boys out gathering more wood and furze for the fire.

She could hear them, curiously isolated by the high bank of pebbles behind her.

She felt the evening in herself, a transfiguration of time and matter as though none was separate from the other, all were joined inseperably thinking evening and it was coming to pass.

Perhaps at such a moment someone thought of Aphrodite stepping on to a golden shore, and she was there, leaving the flaring shell lifting on a wondering sea.

If I close my eyes, does it go on, she thought. Shall I miss some changing somewhere, and must it be time forward. Might it not be time retreating. Does it happen because it comes of its own, or is selected by a higher one, or does it come because I think it. Does the sea sleep in secret when we sleep, or does he stir and roll when we wake. Should that shell be turned over by the tide, *Now,* did it or the sea do it, or did you change it forever by thinking it.

Once it is moved it can never be turned back.

So powerful was the sensation of oneness, of utter humility and complete union, that Selene found herself desolate, with an immense compassion for all things.

She heard steps. The moment passed. It seemed as though she had returned from a strange place, empty, a little cold. She rubbed her face against her knees. She felt stiff, the sands cold and lifeless, the warmth gone.

Miceal stood behind her on the dunes. Seeing the men away, he had not liked to go near the tents where the two other girls he could now see were inside the coloured one. Selene looked up. Hello, Miceal. The others will be back soon, come and sit down here until supper's ready.

See the shark there. If he comes into the bay maybe they'll be out for him.

Miceal pointed out the great dark form cruising close inshore off the rocks, the oiling water unbroken by the sliding bulk. The tall, instantly frightening black fin slit the surface of the sea as it slit the membranes of the mind, releasing a shoal of terrors. Still in the ancient armour of his million-centuries' construction, the shark slid unchanged into the changed minds of men, who still contain their fishes' archetypal nightmare.

That one's harmless, it's a basker. Miceal sat down on the stones.

The great fin lay over, turned to a thin sword, swirled and vanished. The water humped glassily.

Henry, Stew and Ran strung back, carrying and dragging their hauls. Ran had outdone the others, staggering under a boat's timber from the beach and an old otter-board lost from some trawler.

Go on up Miceal, I'll be with you in a minute when I've got my shoes on. Selene brushed and dusted the sand from her feet, her sandals beside her on the pebbles.

55

Miceal climbed up the ridge, and Britt called to the others. Oh good, here's Miceal. Everything's ready, boys, so sit down and we'll eat now.

She was very pretty, Miceal thought. Against her pink dress her pale hair and brown skin made her look like a flower.

Letty came out of the coloured tent carrying a plastic bowl of soapy water which she hurled over the furze bushes behind them. I wish you wouldn't do that, it's dirty so near us. OK Granma. She stood combing back her boy's hair from her ears, her washed head small like a wet rat's.

Her dress was trellissed with black, in each square a red rose. Miceal knew something wasn't right there, but could not tell why he felt it. The dress was too harsh for Letty, who had neither the colouring nor the character to carry it.

Selene appeared over the ridge, yawning. She had a man's white shirt over the long red skirt, her hair very black against it, and the rolled sleeves too big for the thin, dark brown arms. She was the dark brown of some old polished wood, he thought; funny how the girls were all different browns, Britt a gold like honey, and Letty like copper, more a red. You are very brown, he said, not easy with talk. You've not caught that in Ireland.

They laughed, and Britt ladled out the plates of stew in the tent's shelter. They hung a black enamel kettle over the replenished fire for tea to come.

No, we've all been in France before we came over here.

We all met camping, and Stew was going anyway to look up some of his ancestors in Tipperary, weren't you, Stew.

So we thought we'd all come too, we've never been

to Ireland. Ran's showing us around. We've not long now though before some of us have to go back.

The boys had second helpings, not waiting for the girls to finish. Miceal refused their offers of more. The new trousers he'd put on for the visit were uncomfortably tight.

Selene sat beside Ran, one hand keeping her hair back. Ran rolled a cigarette, belching happily.

Yes, my wild Thessalian mare, you've beaten us all. A nice rich dark bay. Any more and you'll be a liver chestnut. Oh ha ha. Selene passed a mug of tea to every one. Ran peered into his. I hope it's a good palomino this time. That tin of milk was off at dinner and turned mine a nasty dun. How do you take your Przevalski, Mr. Hennessy, with or without kumiss?

Oh shut up, Ran. She gave him a sudden, surprisingly hard jab in the chest with her fist. I don't think of horses all the time.

No, love. The rest of the time you are one. He curled away from her, protecting his mug with one arm, the other over his head.

She did nothing, drawing her knees up and settling her skirt round her ankles, sipping her tea with both hands round the big mug.

Ran lay where he was, his back to her, and rolled himself another cigarette.

Sure, there's nothing wrong in liking the horses. Miceal addressed himself to the no man's land of the fire.

Ran turned back, his head propped on one hand. She can do anything with them, Mike, anything at all. It's uncanny. She'll be on that white soon, and now that spotted marvel's arrived there's no knowing what she'll be up to. She can't take her eyes off him. Although I admit he's a bit special. In fact, he's bloody fantastic.

Well, at least I know why I love horses, I love them, love them. And I don't care a fuck for what any of you think.

Her face glowed in the fire. Miceal was shocked and half in admiration. Henry winked at him. He coughed and groaned loudly. Oh dear, my father's dun become a little horse today.

Selene was up like a tiger. She threw the mug into the bushes and stormed over at them. Will you all shut up. *Shut up.* Her hair seemed to writhe in the firelight.

Gee, will you look. Stew sat up abruptly. She looks like the Medusa! Lenie, do that again, it's just terrific.

Oh don't say that, Henry cowered dramatically. Or she'll give birth to Pegasus any minute.

Will you shut up.

Anyway you'll have to cut her head off first.

Stew was expressionless behind the bland mask of his glasses.

Britt was troubled. Ah, Lenie. Don't take any notice of them, they're a rotten lot.

Selene turned quickly and ducked into the girls' tent. I'm going for a last swim.

Britt followed her down on to the pale sands, luminous as a pearl under the dark bowl of the sky. The sea wandered and re-formed heavily and quietly like spreading milk.

They made up the fire and Letty fetched a jersey from the tent. I could do with some more tea. She filled the kettle and collected the mugs. I can't see Lenie's anywhere.

Don't worry. Henry hooked up the kettle. We'll look for it tomorrow.

Miceal passed his cigarettes round.

Why do you tease her about the horses?

Henry laughed, pulled on his cigarette deeply, looked

up at the glowing end against the sky. Seriously. He was thoughtful. She's a queer girl. She's Greek, as she probably told you. I don't know if that's got anything to do with it or not, but her family was killed in an earthquake and she was adopted. By a very rich couple, I believe. They told her they didn't know who her father was, which was a bloody stupid thing to do, as the kid was too young to realise that human beings must have human parents, and thought all sorts of odd things. One day she went into the stable and saw a beautiful black horse and thought. Ah, that's my father. With a start like that, and being brought up with them as the only real things in her life, it's no wonder she became fixated on them. You know, she prefers them to us, really. Well except Ran here. And he's a horse of a different colour. Sorry. Ran threw a stick at him. No, she's a marvellous girl really, Mike. Fearfully intelligent too. But she gives me the creeps sometimes, she sort of knows things, before and after, if you know what I mean. That again may be because she's Greek, or what she went through, or something.

Britt returned from the sea. It's lovely down there, as warm as anything.

Ran belched again. That was a lovely meal, pretty Britty. Trouble is the onions. I shall fart all night. You can bloody well sleep outside the tent tonight. Stew's glasses flashed. Brother, the last of your Liffey specials! It's a wonder you don't float outa the place altogether, sleeping-bag and all.

Alright, Moosejaw, if ye don't recognise the odour of sanctity. Ran lifted one leg deliberately, and they all cowered away.

Oh stop it, boys. Honestly!

Britt was supported by Letty. You're a filthy lot, I don't know why we stick with you.

59

Miceal found it easiest to let their talk and sudden departures and arrivals run over him like the tide around rocks. They were strange, fascinating, uncouth, and amazing creatures. He was uncomfortable with them in the sort of way wool is on a hot day, and yet they were easy, he need not feel guarded nor confined with them.

He had a vision of Father Muldoon going up like a brush fire. Jesus, if he could hear some of the things, there's be holy water out and bucketing damnation.

They sat in silence. The kettle whispered the first bars of its boiling whistle.

Miceal wondered if the shark would still be in the bay tomorrow. Perhaps others with it, for the big baskers were seldom alone. No doubt the men of Portrain had already decided to take him: the viewing of one in close was never unmarked for long.

Where's Selene. Britt jumped up. Mike, that shark we saw.

No, no. There's no harm in them, they're baskers.

Ran said she's likely gone for a walk up the strand, you know what she is.

Britt was troubled. She ducked into the tent and came out struggling into a black high-collared jumper. I'll walk along the top and see if I can see her.

She won't thank you if you disturb her on one of her lone jaunts, you know. Stew rubbed his hands, pushing scattered sticks back into the fire. He broke up some furze, cursing at the prickles.

Well, I'll go slowly towards the village and back down the sands. Her white daisyhead of hair disappeared into the dusk.

The fire flamed and the kettle huffed its lid. From the curved spout a thin pencil of steam scrawled on the darkness.

Letty made the tea, the congregation of square white mugs clustered together solid and helpless as fat women. The big brown tea-pot crowed over them like a triumphant preacher. For what we're about to receive, the spout bending unctuously above them. Fill our hearts and minds with the knowledge of thy heavenly tea. Amen, said the mugs.

They sipped the tea slowly. It was wood-flavoured from the fire. Miceal said You should see the men from Portrain take the shark tomorrow should it be still in the bay. A great sight in this island, and not much done now at all.

He told them of the netting and the battle with the great fish, the men in the shining black currachs hounding and worrying it closer to the shore, the powerful tail hacked through and the great witless head lanced again and again until the dim mind returned to water. It would be towed into the little harbour, and hoisted by chains to stretch Portrain between its ruined ends, and still dumbly moving. The fishermen would leave it with the curious compassion of the victors over the vanquished, for the tourists to prod and stare and surmise, the children to be photographed by the alien eye which could only measure oceans.

I wrote a poem once about it, Ran said unexpectedly. I came here as a lad and saw them go after one while I was out fishing. Did you know Mike, this island looks just like a shark's fin seen from the sea. You can't see the island, just the Coolnay mountain going straight up and down out of the sea. It's as though the place draws the sharks or vice versa. He looked into the fire, his thin face gentle suddenly.

No Athenian dawn, this.
No homespun cockerel
Kindles both worlds to light.
But the meagre ass
Rends day from night
As though the dawn aborted.
And the black island dropped stillborn.
From bended heads of land,
Butting Atlantic like an angry goat,
Men watch the amethyst and emerald,
The sapphire, crafty sea.
Who waits on one of them.
To take him from his hearth, his field of stones,
And to fashion his bones
Into a basalt image in the rock.
His eyes crystalline with visions,
His finger-bones, sea-lilies.
To toy him on her lulling, spongy bed
And flood and keel and gulf him for her own.

And the great shark sliding
Into the mind of the bay
Like a dark thought.
An unbidden apparition
Channelled by the seas' chambers,
And the alchemy of years
Into men's profoundest fears.

And he is taken in the wily nets
That enclose and straighten him
As reason holds and deciphers the black dream.
The spears work their calvary, and his dim mind drowns
In the mantle of red he lays at the seas' door.

He sags in ruin on the warty stones,
On land, his vast anatomy
A mere indecency of bulk to the intrigued observer,
Who prods the fled eye
And imagines lust and murder, ravenings and Jonah.
Not knowing that this was a formal, ordered fish,
Who with portalled jaws as wide as dolmens
Rollered and hammocked down his sea leagues
Without haste, and with economy and virtue.

A sluggard, big and witless as a house,
With nothing on his mind but a sea-louse.
Who would gag on anything
Bigger than a shrimp, so help him.

His tenant lice, hastening from their cold companion,
Scrawl an aimless, scratchy tribute,
Unreadable, to his memory.
But however they may laugh and pry,
How many of those clustered at his side
Could be like him, so vast in life and death
That even without an epitaph
He is his own monument?

Aye. Miceal lit a cigarette thoughtfully in the silence. Aye, that's it right enough.

He felt the grey, bleak life of his compared with theirs; beasts and weather, the slow heavy tread of time, his thoughts penned always like the sheep, and his tongue held like a bull by the brow-chain.

Ran brought out a guitar and they all sang with him. Miceal envied them their ease.

Now, flamenco. Please, Ran. Do you know flamenco, Mike? No, I'm sorry.

It's the music of the Spanish gypsies, no use trying to sing it. You make a balls of it if you haven't the kind of voice for it, and I haven't.

Ran drew the guitar into him, hooding over it, like a hawk on its kill.

Miceal was bewildered and shaken by the lure and fierceness of the music. It seemed to writhe in the fire, to lead you into ice and burning so that the hairs crawled on you like a dog's. He felt a new country of the spirit lying before him as a traveller, yet was afraid to leave the island of himself.

The occasional dance, the traditional bands, the ballads and the radio, these were straight roads enough, this other a path which if you stepped on it would turn like a snake and fang you. To dance would be to partner the world's most beautiful woman with snakes in her hair.

Miceal was breathing hard.

Ah-ha. Britt's voice came out of the darkness triumphantly. They looked round, Ran laying the guitar aside and gulping the last of his cold tea. She was signalling to someone behind her. Into the firelight rode Selene, coaxing and kneeing the white horse who stepped nervously and stopped, shrinking, eyeing the fire with his head tipped. He sighed and blew at the smoke, his nostrils tight with dislike, evading contact and knowledge of it. Selene was as black as the mountain behind her head, her shirt and the white horse shining flamingo pink in the firelight, and from where they sat looking up, his eye and the evening star sparking together in the night sky.

Commander Fay of the Fortyfirst reporting. Stew's ironic Canadian cracked the silence. They all laughed and the horse jumped. Selene slid off and removed the rope from his head and mouth. He stood by her as she unknotted and re-wound it. He shook his head, then braced himself and shook himself all over with a shuddering like wet blankets in a wind, his loose ears slapping like gloves.

He looked at her for a moment, turned and walked away with his tail swinging, into the darkness.

So that's what you were at. And we poor lads thought you'd been swep' away by a ravenous porbeagle.

I knew he'd be easy to catch now his place has been taken. He was glad in a way for the attention. He was quite near, standing all by himself behind that empty hut.

Was he wild with you? She looked on fire in the red skirt.

Oh no, he's been broken to harness as well, he's full of old harness marks.

You looked just like a Gauguin, sweetie, so did your pink horse. Henry's voice was lazy and affectionate.

I think I'll be making a move now. Miceal got up awkwardly. Bloody trousers, Jesus he was crippled. Henry jumped up.

Tell you what, let's drop in at the pub on the way. We'll walk back with you Mike, I want to get some beer in for tomorrow. I'd forgotten we'd completely run out when you came. Shame on us, and a good Irishman to supper, too.

Will you come in for a quick one?

The girls decided to come as well.

Where shall we go? That first one looks a bit dingy. What's it like, Mike? 'Tis all the old country men go there, there's not the life in it at all.

Well, if it's deadly we could all go on to Feeney's.

Aye, ye'd best do that, I'm thinking.

On the way they passed the white horse, standing in the shelter of the furze-bushes near the tents. He nukkered gently to them. Selene unconsciously answered him as she would answer one of them in conversation. The others teased her. She saith Ha ha among the trumpets, neither turneth she back from the sword! The glory of her nostrils is terrible. Ow, no, no Lenie, I give up. Honestly. No, I promise. Oo you cow, that hurt. They scuffled and ran in the darkness.

They tramped into the dimly lit, musty little room of

the first bar, a smell of chickens and sawdust whineing in with them through the door.

A gloomy row of the established had stabled themselves along one wall, and Miceal remembered suddenly those evenings when nothing was said at all but Good luck now, Pat. Sound, man, sound. Ye're looking well, and Good-night all, with no movement beyond a slow tramp for replacements up to the bar and another out of the back to make room for more. At least there was talk tonight. He could hear an unbroken zoom like hornets going in and out of holes, and the high sporadic moo of old John Tuohy.

BrummmOmm. Bummrha. Hermummon. *Mahr*. Buddlyboomummunnard. Wassoimmardomm. *Mahr*. Ayedyseendumman. *Mahr*.

Like a row of snails the old men immediately retracted their conversation, humped their shells back again and drew in their horns of communication.

Their examined their boots and the floorboards, the walls and their suddenly hypnotic glasses.

The younger men's eyes darted like pike at the girls, snapping them up with gulps of Guinness and scaling away their clothes, leaving the lovely livebait women flashing and wriggling in the middle of the imagination's floor. Arragh said Tady McCann and they all knew what he meant.

Miceal felt embarrassed, ashamed, he was surprised none of the others seemed to notice anything wrong, they wore their usual natural good humour.

A few forced, hearty remarks, and both sides withdrew. When they went it seemed to the snails, now pulsating with conversation, as though the gloom was worse than ever.

Lord, what a morgue. We might've been from another planet. Stew was amazed.

66

They christened it the Neanderthal Arms.

Did you see the way they looked at Lenie.

Ran quoted. Warrented quiet and fruitful, only for sale as no-one can ride her.

For full trial over jumps apply Mrs. Queenie Sheba, Moabite Villas. Macaughthepox, County Havaslygo.

They walked through the darkened, empty village towards Feeney's.

Lit up like a big square boat on the edge of the rocks, Feeney's was full of tourists and singing. A fat woman walrused herself on to a table top and hoofed on it like a skittish Clydesdale.

Ballad singers with their eyes in prayer dirged in corners among their devotees, and Kevin Barry was fervourdly tortured by a local baritone.

The English visitors received glares and embrocations of hatred well rubbed in during the performance.

The noise was overpowering, and they all stood for a moment by the door adjusting themselves.

Seven times Kevin surged like a fire siren, and the Lark rose in the clear air from another corner. Paddy McGinty's goat was twanged along by a Belfastman with a voice like a Jew's harp, and the fat woman, with the roar of a punctured Zeppelin, fell voluminously on to her embarrassed little husband.

Well, we'll see a bit of fun here. As he said it, Miceal felt wrong. What the hell was the matter. He'd always thought Feeney's a grand place for a jar and a bit of song, a grand place for a hooley in the season.

Now he saw the red sweating faces, the stupidity, the randy vacancy. Spilt beer and broken glass, the long pink shiny knickers and the varicose veins of the fat woman. He felt sick. They ordered drinks. He wanted to apologise again, but the boys were easy, drinking and joking together, the girls as graceful as deer

67

amongst the other flushed women in the room, not consciously apart, though not joining in the guffawing and stamping.

The master of ceremonies sank into a pint at a quiet moment, and the boys suddenly sang together. They drew the listeners quietly to their faces as they sang in Gaelic first, then in Welsh, English and Spanish. There was a silence when they ended, then the everyday masks were in place again, and they were cheered. Britt was seized by Smirky, who cantered her round by the shoulders as though she was a wayward heifer on a halter. Come on girls, dance. Everybody dance. A solemn lad with his hair standing out like a moulting spring ass placed himself in front of Selene and glassily looking through her, battered the floor in a step dance. His bright red ears stuck out like frosted brussel-sprouts.

He suddenly finished, bowed to her like someone practising in a mirror and weaved away to the bar. Britt managed to eel out of Smirky's grasp and got behind Selene, laughing and gasping. She pushed her forward. Come on Lenie, you dance. What about music. Someone at the piano began a tinny tango. No, no music. Someone else put out most of the lights, there were cheers. Selene looked dazed for a moment. She went over to the fireplace, the men making way for her, and took down two blackthorn sticks which hung above it. They were curiously twisted. She slowly held them out in front of her stiffly. *Duende* said Ran softly, clicking his fingers and whistling with a haunting, subtle rhythm. He seemed to direct her through someone unseen.

The ghost, you must wait for it to come. Henry spoke in a low voice. Miceal understood in his heart. We never know how Lenie'll start, or what she'll do. You just go with her. Watch, she's really something.

68

Slowly Selene danced, the long red skirt in flames around her, her face withdrawn, her gaze inward. She drew on something deep within herself. In her hands the blackthorn sticks began to move and writhe, to come alive, a trick of the shaking firelight and their own curves. Miceal felt his eyes dry and staring. He blinked. At the end, she flowed down into the spreading red skirt like a flame failing, the sticks and her black hair coiling into each other like snakes in the dim light. It was as though she had disappeared, leaving a dead fire in the middle of the floor.

Ran had ended exactly with her.

Let's go, Henry said. They went before the lights were switched on again, before the outburst of cheers and the calls for more.

Pity the dress wasn't quite right. Henry grinned at her. They'd have all gone quietly berserk.

Yes, but weren't those sticks exactly like snakes.

Exactly like, my little bit of Cretan crackling.

They were off again, their verbal hares leaving him stranded like an old dog, Miceal thought.

Funny he knew what her dance was, explanations were not needed. The date, the civilization were things for the chronicles and knowledge, the dance and the dancer for the older heart.

Blast. After all that we've forgotten the beer.

He left them where the roads divided, standing and listening to them as they turned down the track towards the strand. They had decided to walk back along the sands, the holes and stones on the dunes being hazardous in the dark. Calls. Come again, Mike. See you soon. Promise. He promised. Britt's sandals were loose and clicked as she walked.

Like one of our own reindeer she had said.

Henry had his arm around Letty, and she was walking barefoot, carrying her shoes.

Their conversation circled back to him like smoke, fading into the low murmur of the sea.

As he reached the croft the collie shook himself, and the chain rattled the nerves in the still air. A new moon was falling back into the sea, her tail already in it. Like a curved and shining fish so that you waited to hear the splash.

She's like a big hen salmon tonight, thought Miceal. She'd arch and beat as you took her, clean and silver with her run through the sky, her eye angry and dismayed until blooded by the priest. Strange how fish look when fresh from the sea, no-one would guess how alive the eyes, and so angry, how vivid the rainbow of their bodies, how violent their protest at the choking world of men as they drown in the air as surely as men gasp under their green skies.

If you knocked her down now into the boat, to quiver and arch by your boots, beating herself stiff as the boards, would the light die with her there in the bottom of the boat, or would your hands shine in the night where you'd taken her.

And what if you'd killed her light altogether and you with only a few scales left in your hand.

A fin of light and the moon rolled under.

And sheltered by the furze-bushes the band of horses dozed and grazed at the night, nibbling the tips off the hours, grazing time bare with their long yellow teeth.

Some standing about like tombs to a fallen civilisation, a black asleep on his side like an overturned boat, a luminous dun resting like a closed moth.

70

The mizzen-star was asleep, his own moons and constellations moving with his slow breathing, his dappled coat stretched out as though a bit of sky was pegged down among the bushes.

Clouds veined in from the west to marble the sky's hide like his own, but the big horse still slept on, his fringed mane laid out on the ground like a shawl.

Miceal went often to suppers by their fire.

On his way back with the cows or from looking over the sheep, he would drop in a load of sticks for them, or if there had been a sheep killed, some cuts from it wrapped in newspaper and left in the tent if no-one was there.

Sometimes he spent a day taking them round the cliffs to the seal caves at the northern end of the island, and they were surprised how fast and sure-footed he was in his heavy boots over the rocks, while they struggled to keep up with him.

The girls brought packages of food with them, but he seldom ate anything, accepting a beer if pressed, but obviously unused to eating in the day.

He did not take them up to the croft. They were not part of the life up there, there was nothing to see but the fowl and the white walls, even the beasts roamed out most of the year. He was surprised at their delight when they came on his three asses by the lake. Oh Miceal, you didn't tell us you had donkeys. Aren't they heavenly, what do you use them for? They thought the island carts unnecessarily heavy for the small asses, and Selene was highly critical of the assortment of ropes and chains that made up their harness.

Don't you ever cut their feet, Miceal? You'd be

71

prosecuted in most places for letting them get so bad.

He didn't want them at the cabin. It was his hole in the mountain, like the fox's. He was safe to himself there, his own smell was on it. He was afraid of its untidiness in their eyes, although he kept it in as good order as any woman. They understood his reluctance.

Gradually he came to sit with them and walk with them more and more, listening to their songs and arguments with a greater ease. There was little to do at the croft with the hay saved and the corn still green as shallow water. He brought them milk in a white enamel can, white milk from the black cows, and eggs, each one wrapped in a tear of paper.

The collie was quiet with them, accepting their pattings with his ears pressed back, his eyes on Miceal's face. He was no part of them, only alert to slot himself at Miceal's heels as soon as he moved.

They wanted to spend one day on the rocks under the Bull's Head. There were curious and beautiful colours there, pale green marbles, the purples of pophory and amethyst, and the dark reds of jasper and carnelian. The black basalt Bull stretched his head under the sea at high water for nearly a mile. At low tide you could walk on his face, crinkled and whorled with sea-lilies, and look down into the depths where his chin rested on the sea-bed among pastures of waving weed.

His horns, ringed with the millions of his ageing, held the sea open between them like the poised claws of a scorpion.

That day they saw a large company of basking sharks travelling slowly at their feet, all with their vast mouths gaping wide as doors, their fleshy trunks turned back like charging elephants. The silence of the great gathering was uncanny. Somehow you expected a vast noise,

72

bassooning among the trundling bodies. Silence, and the small green pebble eyes of indifference.

How strange we can see them. Henry was frowning. Something like this must have happened millions of times for millions of years, and men's eyes never saw it. D'you know what I mean? It's as though us seeing them has invented them, somehow. They don't know what they are, we do. Dinosaurs must have looked and moved in the same way. They were there. All that fearful unconsciousness. It's terrifying somehow.

They must have looked at each other, the lizard eyes. I can't explain it properly. A terrible blind unawareness. Under the hot sun.

The egg cracked and oblivion crawled out and no one saw it. No one said Look, that's a dinosaur. Oh my God. He seemed shaken.

All that long crawl into us, that fearful, blind, relentless dying upon dying to give us minds. Before God, perhaps. It went on and on until we said one day O good now I'm God I can remember all this, and we could look at each other and see. Know. Damn, *oh damn.*

Miceal was afraid. Henry was mad, this was surely the talk of the devil. Ran ruffled his hair, sat down beside Henry. It's no use raging against the sea. The girls were silent. The seas and all that in them is. And God said Let us make Man.

Selene and Britt. They were so different, yet alike in their difference. Letty wasn't the same. She was like sheep in a flock. Miceal watched them swimming and playing. Talking and walking. The grace of them, the spirit. No women he'd met were like these two shining

73

girls, Britt so lovely, like a flower or a day of sun.
Selene. There was a dark tide, a feeling like that round
the rocks by the Bull's Head. He couldn't explain, only
felt it, the dark and the light. The laughter and the sea.

Would he swim or drown.

Yet the sea might throw you up like the dying
porpoise, and the sun crack you into stone.

Which has the dark and which the light, when night
and day had both, indivisible. And a man neither the
sun nor the moon.

Miceal puzzled and questioned. Everything he knew.
Or did he know. What now were lies. Truth like a
thick broth, badly cooked. God and the devil. Britt and
Selene. The unholy Catholic Church. The stupidity of
the saints and the life everblasting. I confess my sins.
Britt and Selene above all others. Heaven and earth,
the time of the long lizards, Pongo and Pan in the
garden of Eden and who apes who.

The banana of everlasting Amens.

And God created an immaculate misconception, now
and at the hour of our death, Amen.

Father Muldoon was taking his evening stroll along the
dunes. He took long side to side strides like a searching
raven, prodding into the hollows of the evildoers whom
he hoped to catch. Up and down on the switchback of
righteousness, he flapped for balance on the promon-
taries, his black crow-eyes pinpointing the next likely
lair of corruption.

Don't-be-lookin'-down Muldoon, the terror of Aranchilla's youth. Yeh must not be lookin' down. Yeh must not be touching it with the hand at all. Take it in yeh handkerchief lad, and do not be lookin' at it the while. Evil thoughts. We must be prepared against the impure thoughts. But Father. No buts. There's not one but to it. Last time I pissed in me shoe. Ye'll say a Rosary.

With yeh handkerchief. And don't be lookin' down. Good evening Miceal.

Good evening Father, yeh gave me a start.

If yeh were not doing or thinking wrong ye'd have no fear. I do not like the company ye have, Miceal. Not at all. Ye must beware of the temptations of the wicked. The devil works in many disguises, Miceal. The dog looks well, praise God.

Don't be forgetting 'tis Sodality Sunday now. Ye'll be at confession. Aye, Father I will. Good, good. Good dog.

Good-bye now, Miceal. All the best, Father.

Peck peck down among the tourists. An eye here, a couple of maggots there. Bedad, nearly missed that nice bit of carrion. In the bathing suit they call it. Whores' raiment, *cronk*.

Don't wait until they're dead, don't wait for the whites of their eyes. To turn up. *Prruk*.

It was not a sudden thing. It came like the snake, slowly edging through his mind's grass. The grass springing back so that you would say nothing had changed, nothing to see. But it had been, seen or unseen. Whether an alien or a natural thing, according to the observer, it was still part of its ecology; the same law in the ecology of the mind. It was like a light going, a growing disharmony of thought and action.

Miceal found himself unreasonably angry with the fire in the first morning, the kettle for its wilful slowness. And the cows, once part of his quiet and leisurely hours, now a burden and an aggravation. He shouted at the beasts with sudden bursts of spiked anger, yet suffered with them from the sudden unexpectedness and violence which tore out of him like a savage dog when the chain breaks. His hair fought the comb, and he broke both. Shaving was a contest with himself as opponent and referee. If he cut himself he wanted to cut again, and deeper, to ·fight the dark face staring unhappily from a being slowly becoming a stranger to itself.

Eating at aunt Minna's was a physical motion only, cardboard and shell would have tasted as well to him. He began to walk with a low head, his body drawn, eyes unwilling to look too long. Uneasy in company as the wolf is with a stranger, uncertain whether to challenge or to cringe acceptance with the bent neck. The sun shone, and he knew it was there, but it might be black for the pleasure of it was gone.

It had once folded himself and the beasts and the island in a round light, now it was as though a candle behind a grey blanket at the broken window.

The moon took him in a cold hand and shook him at night, and the stars stared at him with the insane glitter some travelling men carry in their eyes. His dreams fell out onto the bare floor like coins from empty trousers. He was desperately ashamed at what he dreamed, awoke sweating, and dreamed of worse.

He did not go near the strand, and looked down on the sea crawling like a lizard over stones. He knew what it must be as a ghost, this being worse as he knew he was alive.

76

He drank and fell like Paul on the road, and cried for blindness if it would mean revelation.

The mountain turned from him and cut him with the white rock, and sea-birds warned him on the cliffs, ravens sidled intently where he lay, watching his eyes.

He prayed to the faded and chipped little figure of the Queen of Heaven. Her theatrical rosebud face offered him no release nor comfort. Why. Why. He knew when he returned while the cows were yet waiting for him in the early mist. The cat had a mouse by the door. Twisting and writhing slowly as if through water she langoured, sensually rolling in the pleasure of her prowess, suddenly stiffly spastic at an imagined escape, crucified with frenzy.

The mouse was lightly hooked back from the easy death, a shivering pendulum tossed and returned between the indecisive claws. A zealous judgment, and the teeth were into his spine. The cat cleaned and settled herself into neatness above him.

Miceal stood looking down at her and she yawned up at him, her eyes tigering for a moment before veiling them to the benign slits which, like all cats, she presented to the world of men. The body of the mouse lay like an old man bent over in prayer, the pink forepaws close together beside the pointed nose, from which hung a bead of blood. He grinned as though he had incisored death and found it cheese.

Miceal knew he wanted the two girls on the strand, the fair and dark. Both.

Holy Mother of God he said as he opened the door. And the claws to come.

They came up the mountain to look for him, the girls concerned that he might be ill.

The boys pulled at leaves and hit at long grass, bleating at the sheep with hoarse voices like rams. The old ram with his tarred face and handled horns ignored them, rubbing his full-fleeced behind on a rock, his Roman nose rocking against the sky. Shorn ewes like skinny white rats on black matchstick legs prodded about the turf, contrasting with the unshorn with their tattered grey blankets bouncing at each step like shaggy concertinas. An occasional startling human cough *Euff-ffa,* and a rattling liquid belch of a bleat as a mother called to her lamb through a mouth stuffed with wind, cud and grass. The lambs, white, round and complete, only lacked the wooden wheels of Victorian childhood and a string for pulling.

They watched a black lamb with a chocolate mousse coat kneeling under its angular mother, butting and jigging its catkin tail like a small boy fishing.

Miceal's dog saw them coming and foxed at them sharply on his chain. His eyes were like needles, his tail falsely brushing as collies will, even as they snap.

Miceal had lost a calf. They found him by a wall, under which the black cow lay, spent.

The effect of his loss was greater at that moment than their unexpected appearance up the field. The cow raised her head to them, her eyes lost in weariness, her muzzle lined with effort, teeth grinding a bitter cud.

The lifeless calf lay by her tail, sleek and wet as a seal, ears still folded and limp. Its milky eyes looked drowned, the mauve tongue rough as a starfish, the small pronged hoofs still jellied. A sense of waste came to them all.

If it had breathed and then died, it wouldn't have been so bad. The eyes would still contain the amaze-

78

ment, the life and the quickening. Now its darkness was complete, not even journeying from one darkness to another, but drowned in its beginning.

A bull, said Miceal, showing them the small empty purse between the long legs.

They helped him to pull the calf away and into the byre.

The cow was up when they returned, anchored with the afterbirth at her heels. She was aware of loss and bewildered, unable to release the chains of reaction, the nosing and licking, the gentle communication, the pride and the peace which crown the hearts of beasts at this moment, and which curiously reward those of men who witness it. With quick, agitated steps, ears funnelled for the calf's bawl, the cow came nervously into the byre, swinging round defensively as Miceal quietened her. He pushed against her bony hip until he had her in place, and fastened the chain round her neck. Hay was in front of her and she snatched a wisp, then swung her head and lowed softly at him, her hollow flanks ballooning.

What will you do with the calf, Miceal. Britt was sad. Nothing. It will go to the dogs around.

He didn't want them at the croft now. He could meet them on the nomansland of the shore, but now was like a dog with strangers in his home, stiff and spiked with unease. He knew they could overlook its plainness and disorder but he did not want the intrusion of their eyes. The old shawl-blanket on his bed, and the bed he had moved from the bedroom to the kitchen so as to be near the fire, he didn't want them carrying away the image of privacy with them. Something of him, something he wanted to keep in himself, would then be theirs.

He told them he had much to do, and they quickly

agreed. He felt bad then, and offered them tea. With a sudden disorder in their skein of friendship, a tangling which when unwound can sometimes leave only an emptiness, they all tried hard to be as natural as before, to show nothing was wrong.

Careful how they went like cats on a greenhouse roof.

The fire was stacked with peat, and Miceal hooked the kettle over it, the kettle disappearing behind the surging smoke like a magician. It would take a time before the fresh peat caught and reddened.

He searched the cupboard for matching cups. They would have it outside in the sun, they said. It's such a lovely day to be indoors. Respecting his privacy and feeling better themselves.

He felt rather than heard the figure in the doorway. He turned to face Paudi, his blue eyes narrow as a cat's, a suitcase on the step.

Holy Mother, man. Yeh set the heart across me.

They looked at each other coldly. You'd best come in. Paudi smiled. And what's the hard man himself been at then. 'Tis the visitors now, is it. What's on here brother, the Mountain Dew Cafe, is that it. That black-haired one, Jesus. Miceal spat inwardly. I like 'em with the mane long, man. Yeh can throw 'em and hobble 'em well with it, if need be. Well, yeh look the same, but who's the party, our Mick.

Miceal told him shortly, while Paudi sat at the table rolling a cigarette and watching the others through the open door. When the tea was ready they cut up some brown bread and buttered it and carried it out between them, Miceal bringing a faded lace tablecloth his mother had used for best. The girls protested they should have been allowed to help, and Paudi grinned at them like a fox. This is my brother, Paudi.

80

The uneven picnic ended with Paudi singing and all feeling more at ease.

Come down to supper, Miceal, and bring Paudi. You haven't been down for ages and we'd love to see you. We thought we'd annoyed you or something. No, I'd work in hand and they wanted some beasts taken to the fair up the road from here. I'd no chance 'till now.

Oh good, well we'll see you both tonight. Thanks for the tea Miceal. They had thought the butter horrible, very strong and rancid, as though the cows had been eating fish or seaweed.

Shall we help you carry the things in. No. He nearly jumped on them. No, no, that's alright now. The brother and meself will be doing it. Sure, it's no trouble at all. OK. See you then.

Blast and damn it. He hadn't wanted to go down there again yet. Damn Paudi. And a smell in the weather coming, the sun looking washed.

They picked up their things, then stood by the side of the cabin watching the figures go down the mountain quickly like sticks into a bog with the distance increasing. They turned to look at each other, Miceal with distrust, Paudi brittle with laughter. They said nothing, and Miceal walked slowly away to the byre, unhooking a chopper from the back of the cabin. He cut up the calf, putting the joints still covered in the wet black hair into a sack, hanging it on a nail. It would keep the dog for a while. He threw the head at the chained collie, *thok.*

Paudi, the last one he'd wish to see. Like the cuckoo, a short stay and on the wing again, and no place safe from his restless eye.

Paudi lay back on the turf, eyes closed against sun and cigarette, his mind filming a pleasant sequence in

81

which the dark girl was overcome as a colt is thrown when it first feels the rope. The film broke. Bloody dump. But we'll see if there's life in the old place yet. Stand back and let the dogs see the rabbit. That dark one, there was eating and drinking on that one, Paudi me boyo. Devil a bit. Ah, now.

He felt the island trying to take him back, mother stone into his bone. It always happened when he'd been there a short while, you could hear the island trying to get you. Your eyes salt with the sea's looking, the sea-wind in the caves of your belly, birdsong in the thickets of your mind, and the grass nerving into your skin and out again with daisies, the waters of Aranchilla, the many waters spilling through the crystal net of your body. All the heart of the place which bred you, and for which a tree would have leaved herself in winter.

Paudi would not give in, writhing off the hook of memory, and by cutting off the roots of his being he killed the shoots of his living, his growth cut back with perversity's sharp knife.

He liked to think of himself as a bird of passage, but Paudi had not migration's purpose, and the freedom he sang was a repetitive prattle. In a cage he made for himself.

Miceal piled dry fern under the black cow, bringing her another forkful of better hay. He pumped her a bucket of water, and the noise roused Paudi, who lazed up to see what he was doing.

Yeh still at it, then. Why the hell don't yeh give it all up, man. A deal of labour for feck all. It needn't just be Dublin, there's better places than that. The girls for one thing, they're a lot easier across the water. Miceal put the bucket down by the cow's head, and she drank deeply, tipping it with each draught. 'Tis all you think of. Or ever did. And your Faith gone. I wonder you return at all to annoy the heart and soul out of us all.

Aye, I'm a hard man. A hard man.

D'yeh never think of marrying and settling some place.

Ah, I get what I want from the creatures without taking the halter. They're the cheapest in Dublin, ye'll not find them anywhere else the same. A quid and they'll give you the money's worth, I'll say that. And what of you, man, what of our bold brother. If Eileen and yehself wait these many years ye'll be taken to the altar in yeh coffins and neither of yeh even joined. Or are yeh wedded to the beasts. And in more ways than one. Yeh'll end like the man in the story who couldn't leave the cows alone.

And what the hell's that. Miceal still hadn't his meaning.

Yeh don't know it. Well now it's this, Pope Innocent. His dad were worried, got a hold of a tart to try and turn him into other channels, so to speak. O yes, I can cure him, says she. Never fear says she, and trots out in all her finery to the byre to find the lad lying exhausted in a wheelbarrow.

Mr. O'Callaghan, says she. I've come to help yeh. Anything yeh wish just let me know, says she. I'm strong and willing, Mr. O'Callaghan. Strong and willing.

Strong and willing is it, says he. Then be a good girl and wheel me down to that oul' black at the end.

Is that yourself now, Mick, in a couple of years.

Miceal hurled the bucket at him and the cow jumped back, choking on her chain, her eyes bulging.

It clanged and dented down the track where Paudi was jigging from stone to stone.

O go and fuck.

He sauntered off in his red check seaman's jacket to air himself in the village.

How is it then, Paudi. Sound, Mrs. Hannen, sound.

Yeh're looking well, God be praised. Surely, Mrs. Hannen surely. And the same with yehself.

Crab-faced old whore. Only a billy-goat would fancy that one. And not so far wrong at that with all the whiskers on her chin. Maa, Mrs. Hannen. Would yeh like a bit of a comather on me horns.

Tomorrow, thought Miceal, we'll take the sheep over to Coolnay. On the southern end of the island there were a few fishermens' cottages scattered like sugar lumps. The grass was fine even up to the high back-bone of the Bull Rock mountain. A deceptively gentle slope took you up unawares to the great rocks at the top, where you thought to see more to come, only to find yourself balanced on the bull's spine and his black stone head a thousand feet below you in the sea. His muzzle flat in the water, and a white froth around it. Some evenings the froth would be pink, and scuffs off it blow away on the tide, like that from the destroyed black southern bull kneeling in the hot sand awaiting the small, poised crucifix of oblivion. The winds were strong at the top, even on fine days. Tearing, wheeling and changing direction at every gust, so strange and elemental a place there was a legend that the winds were born there, out of a deep rift in the Bull's head.

At a certain stage of high water at a southerly blow, the Bull would roar and bellow until the wind aimed its descabello and the sea choked and bubbled him into silence. Away down on the Kerry coast there were two

84

smaller rocks, the Cow and Calf, and the island story was that once they all grazed the green fathoms together, but the Black Bull was challenged by Maeve's Brown of Cuailnge as it raged over Ireland in its madness. Gored and near death, the Black stretched out on Aranchilla's strand to recover. The tale went that should the Black Bull rise and join them, Ireland would be great again. As a lad Miceal used to see the Bull tear free from his grassy centuries, the little cabins sliding like flies down his stony flanks, his barnacled head whaling up from the sea. And his buried horns, which looking down you could see stretching beneath the sea, rising up through the green acres and scything off the horizon with the sweep of the moon on one tip and the sun hooked up on the other.

Miceal and the collie took up the bigger flock from near the strand and penned them in the yard, and separated his smaller one without trouble from his neighbour's red-marked beasts by the far end of the lake.

It was evening when both lots were together in the yard, a changing patched-blanket of sheep humming and clicking and the odd black and brown among them like a lazy woman's darn. The blue marks on their rumps flecked through them like the weave of a Connemara jacket.

The aunt Minna had pecked up every grain of gossip in the village, and was in full cluck when Miceal called in on his way down to the strand.

She was in her usual state over Paudi's arrival, disapproval and aggravation contesting auntly affection in a tag-match of loyalties to all sides. But as the Faith was called in to referee, a hard and narrow decision prevailed, and affection was headlocked into submission. All of which set the aunt Minna into a greater whirl of agitation. She became more and more brassy and hollow until Miceal thought she'd dong like the school bell. She seemed to swell like a hen, and he thought one day she'd reach the impossibility of containing herself in herself, and *Ploff*, a messy fizz and the aunt Minna will go off like a failed Roman candle.

The rumours, her suspicions, denials and didyeh hears flicked wetly round Miceal's ears like shoals of fish. Scurrilous lies fell into the tea. Something Mrs. Facey heard lumped bitter in the soda bread, the milk winked a weak eye and asked for God's help in the muddy voice of a pious mullet.

Miceal escaped at last, his mind as unquiet as his stomach.

When he reached the long stretch of turf to the strand he saw Paudi's red jacket ahead, dipping over the dunes like a float on water, and God knows what hook he's on. Miceal walked faster.

He heeled down the steep shingle where the stream cut deeply into the turf and edged among the pebbles with a sound like Indian bracelets. The rich bay water shining like a thoroughbred's skin.

Over the sands it fanned out into the sea, pulses of water flowing down it as though from the hearts of its parent lakes. Where both waters met, they frilled and curled back from each other, the sea rolling otter-brown, and the bay river wrinkling at each graze on the salt edges like a horse's lip.

Cream froth blew up the shore and lay on the sandy

neck of the beach, laced with a mane of bubbles, each rolling its own rainbow.

A dead gunmetal conger, its ringed yellow eyes bored with malevolence, a last cold bark gagged in the white throat, lay in the division of the waters. It had been bitten across the neck, and the head glared backwards and forwards as the stream toed it deliberately over into the sea. The sea returned it with a firm push.

The albino lips and thorny grin nigger-minstreled between them with the inane obstinacy of the un-wanted.

A large Jewish gull policing the sands paused by it, circled an examination, then tugged it angrily and un-necessarily down the shore until losing interest and floating into the air off bent legs.

A piccolo of little waders, chittering and tweezing, wittered in front of him on twinkling feet, dipping, beaking and exclaiming, one moment on the wing in a quick arc, so compact together a handkerchief would cover them, then a neatly precise descent and on with their intense quest. They pencilled their interweaving, nervous graphs on the sands, pausing by each stone like small meticulous philosophers in speckled, snuffed frock-coats.

As Miceal approached they whirled away and out to sea, chizzing and piping, erratic as a summer squall, flashing at each turn like a conjurer's cards.

This is myself. I am all this, sea and rocks. Thoughts like birds in his mind. Miceal felt deeply in his heart on the lonely shore. Yet as a man I must separate myself sadly from the little birds and the unseen fish I know live with me now, as I am on this land. I keep myself from the cold eyes of the dead. I am only as the sand, yet in my own form as everything is in its form.

Man is wise, but are not the birds wiser as they fly into life as through death without naming them, but knowing them. Man thought them and invented them. Birth and death. And life a thought between. I cannot rest and say *I am* with quietness, my mind rolls like a bright child's ball over the sea and knows no horizon, no rest.

Man in his knowledge is a cauldron which may crack with the heat, and the alchemy of his mind can spit monsters or create the rainbow as a second God. Yet God rested on the seventh day and man cannot. His last cry must surely be for peace, an eternal drowning in the stars.

Man and stars become God.

Miceal realised he was standing at the sea's edge. O God, how alone, how utterly alone is man. Did God say I've been through this therefore you must suffer too. Or was there only a terrible Unknowing which turned for ever flashing a sightless glare as the lighthouse blinds itself through the night. Eli, Eli. Did he die so desperately as God convulsed with visions, or obstinately as Man, struggling blindly like the roped bull in the slaughterhouse.

Ahead of him Paudi waved to Britt. She rode the white horse down on to the sands, Selene walking beside her. Wonder does Paddy Keegan know his old grey's being used as a beach-donkey. The girls must have sweetened him up somehow, contrary old bugger like his owner. And a damn nuisance 'till they cut him these two years gone now. Fifty guineas they got for him. Wouldn't mind charging that meself for his trade. No foal, no fee, and never mind the guinea to the groom, Mam, yeh pays the fifty and the rest is done for the love of it.

Paudi sniffed happily and smiled round his cigarette.

Go on up to the tents, Paudi. Britt called from the jogging grey. We'll be along in a minute when we collect Mike.

She kicked the horse and bobbed down the strand towards Miceal. Selene followed slowly, walking in the shallows with her skirt held up in one hand.

Look Mike, he's going for us all now. Britt laughed down at him, her fair hair curling under her chin in the wind.

Yeh look well together. He looked up at her smiling, and put his hand on the warm shoulder of the horse. Look, he isn't really white when you see him close to. He's got little speckles all over him. He smoothed the grey neck, flecked and micaed like granite.

We call that flea-bitten, he said. Flea-bitten grey.

Her long bare legs hung loosely against the white barrel, her dress tucked up around her. Like a boy's he thought. A bony kid. He took the horse by the cord around his nose and turned him round.

Selene caught up with them shaking out her skirt as she left the water. Hello, Miceal.

She smiled at him with her head sideways, an odd smile. She looks as though she might make a bit for me, he thought, her brown fingers force his mouth still to see his teeth. A queer look, half smile, half something else, he couldn't tell. He was glad of the horse as a bulwark between them. As though by controlling him he kept her where he wanted her, out of his flesh, yet with his hand still on her.

But unlike other women she was not abashed by his maleness, nor by that of the horse. He was uneasy.

You could watch her as you did an animal moving, she was like an animal, walking naturally and part of the surroundings, as they are. Not like the others who walk about on the land's surface, sticking out and saying I am. Awkward and graceless and without contenting the eye.

Even children without it. Wash your hands. Look, like daddy. Don't do that, it's rude. Blow your nose. Must you do that again.

And the burdens go piling on to their backs and into their minds. Say your grace. And it's gone forever.

The long white mane of the horse curled and lifted with the wind eeling around them in eddies.

He's finer hair than I have. Selene laid a strand of his mane against her black hair. You must be better bred than me, horse.

The horse looked gently ahead with his dark eyes shining through the long white strings of his forelock.

I know. Let's all get on him. We'll get back much quicker, Britt said. Miceal was against it. He might kick. Oh come on, Mike. Be a sport. If we go over to that rock you and Lenie can get up easily. Come on, try. The boys will be amazed.

She guided the horse to a large flat stone and sat back while Selene heaved herself over his withers and took the rope reins. They squeezed up together and made the horse move a pace forward, pulling Miceal up onto his rump. The horse was quiet though uneasy at the extra weight, bunching his tail and lifting his hind legs carefully. The girls were nearly helpless with laughter as Miceal slid about on the shifting hips behind them.

Hold on to me, you goof. Britt called back through her flowing hair. She was clutching Selene. Go on, I won't bite. Hang on tight. He smells different from the boys, she thought. Rough and heather. Oh yes and sheep. Those fearful great boots. I shouldn't think he ever takes them off. His hands took her by the shoulders, carefully.

A cut ran over one knuckle, she saw. Big hands. Her hair blew into his eyes. Hold on everyone, we'll take the boys by storm. Selene kicked the horse into a breathless half trot which rocked them about helplessly until they all urged him into a canter. Shrieking and laughing they bounced down the beach heavily and Selene turned towards the shingle, the horse labouring through the pebbles and up on to the grass, grunting. With the last heave Miceal slid back over the tail and the two girls fell off together sideways. Britt was helped up by the strategically waiting Paudi. Throwing yehself at me now, is it, and me after knowing yeh only this blessed minute.

But they were all laughing so much they couldn't answer him.

Miceal got up stiffly from the knobbly pebbles, rubbing his knees. He found he thought now of Britt as a kid, a laughing kid. Queer, the white horse had shown him something. He felt oddly relieved as though a pain had gone, like the soreness he rubbed from his back and legs. It happened so quickly. One minute he was wanting her, now it had gone, like a blanket pulled off the horse's back he had fallen off in a smack of pebbles, and the want jolted out of him.

He went over to the piled furze and began to make the fire for them. Stew and Henry came in pulling whole bushes between them, and Letty brought out a bag full of newspapers to start it. Ran picked up the trailing rope and jumped up onto the grazing horse. Selene watched him, her knife halfway through the potato she was peeling.

He rode sedately. Like an Etruscan rider, his legs hung down to the little grey's knees. He looked thought-

ful and loose and alone as some do on a horse. He
soon came back, carrying the coiled rope and looking
cold.

The horse nudged along the dunes, and clambered
down into a sandy hollow where it collapsed on to
tucked knees and curled head, rolling with flailing legs,
groaning and thumping among the scattered white bones
of a cow.

Miceal felt the wind coming. He and Paudi warned
them to turn the tents facing in to the island or to move
them in behind the bushes. They knew the quiet weather
was over, the flying moods of Aranchilla. It might
come again, surely, but now wind and rain were in the
air, strong as cabbages.

But the others decided it was too much bother to
pack up and move with the fire and the supper going
well. They were not worried about the tents, they had
stood up to some bad blows before without harm. And
that's just what yeh'll get tonight. Paudi sniffed like a
dog at the sky. Miceal watched the sheep drifting
towards the big lake and its shelter of high whin. He
could see the horses crossing the far ribbon of the road,
where they always grouped in bad weather under
Aranchilla's one dance hall, a gaunt mausoleum which
cracked and peeled leperously by itself and with no
other building within a mile on both sides.

If a hop and a gale came together, and that was
often enough, the horses would watch the fun through
the doors every time they opened. Bang and the light
would yellow out on to the interested faces and winking
eyes. Bang and the night would jump back over them.

You had to be careful not to bull out in a hurry if

you didn't want to run smack into some great hairy arse, and a couple who might escape Father Muldoon's gritty eye would have to choose the wind and the long disapproving faces outside, which soon cooled the most ardent squeezer. However expertly you had her man-oeuvered against the wall, mouths like limpets and a nice handfull of the goods, the most fiery seduction was unlikely to flourish through the attendant cross-fire of farts heralding the subsequent steaming load over your best shoes. For, as Paudi remembered with a grin, the only place out of the damned wind was one small corner by the chimney, and the horses were as deter-mined to keep it as the odd couple was to get there. Tommy Mullins once swore he'd kissed something pretty queer out there in the weather, but sure when you remembered the great whale of a girl he took there, and a face on her like a John Dory, there'd be only the taste of a difference. Miceal saw him watching and thought of his cousin, Eileen. She would try and get him to go to the dances. It was known she was the one. No hurry in these things, but she was for Miceal, they said, nodding. The aunt Minna was as determined as a cow near clover. Eileen knew it and there it rested. Damn the women he thought, hunching his shoulders nearer the fire. But he knew he meant the accepting, unasking women of the crofts, and not the girls who laughed by the sea in the wind's face.

§

The wind-dog of the islanders was well named. It snapped round the tents and pulled out ropes, ran whining round the fire nipping at clothes and hair, chased its tail in circles and like a dog losing interest, suddenly gave up and trotted away. The presence of his master was full of trouble in the air, although he had some green miles yet before he'd crinkle Aranchilla with his smoking lash. The sky rolled along the horizon like a fish's belly, paling bands of green and yellow striped with the warning nimbus like the colours sliding from the dying pike, the sea ruling a metal line beneath it, menacing as an aimed barrel.

As they came to the island the nimbus clouds began to change and reform, flying banners and tails, throwing up heads and horns as they ran on the land to skip and slither over the mountain rocks like tattered goats fleeing the wind-dog.

The wind yelped, veering from the low scenting to the high change of sighting.

Sparks from the fire fanned along the ground like dying fireworks, and they moved the pile of wood back. Britt had decided to finish the meal on two primuses in the tents' shelter when the wind suddenly died. There was an unnatural calm, the sea still bulling and the clouds flighting, but as though the sound had been cut.

Instead of the pushing of the wind there was a drawing-in, a vacuum in the air, a limbo where their voices were flat in the ears and loud.

The action went on like a film with the sound broken down. They felt it would return suddenly with a double force to make them jump. It was the time between the wind-dog and his master, as though something was taking a deep breath to blow out Aranchilla like a birthday candle, rock cake and all off the sea's table.

They ate quickly in the lull, everyone but Miceal and in a lesser way Paudi, more at ease. Miceal felt the coming storm in another layer of his being, it went on despite the talk and himself, like a dog whose nose is this way and the other while he watches you.

Paudi, island bred, felt it too, but it was not his

enemy now, he had more to fear than the wind. We're off in a week, maybe sooner if this weather's breaking. Henry's face switched on as he cupped a match.

Miceal felt a blow inside. As though he was running downhill too fast, the ground unsure. His voice surprised him with its calm. Aye, yeh'll see the others away tomorrow, I'm thinking. A bit of a blow and they're away like the hare and thinking they were mad to come to the powerful place like this. They had retreated into the girls' bigger tent. Letty opened tins of peaches and Britt poured worming stalagmites of condensed milk over each bowl.

No one spoke for a while, chasing the slippery and evasive halves round like soap.

Too big for a comfortable mouthful, they had to be hunted and speared just right, giving the successful pursuer a ridiculous sense of small triumph. Ran clanked his out of the tin, mining the juice up noisily with quick concentration.

Thanks, women. That was grand. They piled the plates into a plastic bowl and put it outside. Britt patted her stomach. I'll wash up later when this lot's gone down a bit. The kettle will stay hot for ages still.

God I'm bloated. Ran belched deeply. *Oxford*! Ran! Sorry my dove. Sheer appreciation.

They all lay back on the girls' bright patterned blankets, the yellow sides of the tent glowing in the darkening air. Stew looked at his watch. There's nearly an hour's difference, last night it was still daylight. He crawled out and looked round the edge of the tent. Holy mackerel, it's like Judgment Day coming on out there.

Oh come in man and don't fuss. Leave it alone and it might go away. Ran lay flat, smoking, behind the girls who had curled up together at the top of the tent, like cats in a chair.

Henry and Stew hunched on one side, sharing smokes, and Paudi eased nearer the girls, his cat's smile whiskering round his cigarette.

His eyes never shared the expression on the rest of his face, they were deliberately curtained to give away nothing.

Only Selene watched him as carefully, though not directly, from the sides of her eyes. Without looking straight at anyone you could talk and laugh without need of the cover Paudi kept over his naked stare. Like a horse you were aware of everything around you. Selene was alert as a hare. Miceal sat near the entrance, part instinct in readiness for the storm, half because living alone made him ill at ease in a crowd.

The silent girls made him sense the sheep smell he felt must be in the warmth of his clothes as the sun brings it out of the flock.

He was slow in his movements from awkwardness in the small space, that he'd knock something with the hurried feeling he had inside, big as an ox in a backyard with the washing. Half with the deliberate slowness you use with a strange beast nervous of you. Much of their talk and banter was still foreign to him, their meanings guesswork.

They had experienced so much more than he could dream of, shut up in his stone box up a mountain. He laughed and puzzled, feeling his own life and the things he knew utterly different and drab, without interest. He didn't know his quietness, his strength in his aloneness, the things he despised in himself were what they admired and reached for in him.

The greatest thing that kept them apart was the barrier his Church put round him. They were beginning to understand, since coming to the island, its grasp, its rigidity, its hold on him. The unquestioning acceptance of its word in all he did or thought, the burden of guilt it presupposed upon him from the cradle. Every damn thing you did was sure to be a mortal sin. Ran said, who had gone his own way. During this last time they all had together, they talked of their lives and their hopes and ideas, beliefs and questionings. They were strangely without fears. Miceal envied them their buoyancy, their refusal to trouble. He tested the future as a man sets over the bog, and trouble yoked you like the ass, the Church teaching acceptance of yet another cross.

At first he had been shocked and disturbed when they discussed religions openly and irreverently, as though playing ball from mouth to mouth. They were amazed at the difference between the uncompromising, rigid brand of Catholicism that gripped Ireland, and that of other countries. They thought it was a fanaticism born of temperament, the greyness of the climate and harshness of the land, and a terrible, secret racial disappointment.

Like a death wish, it wormed through drink and suicide, fear of marriage and emigration. They were saddened at seeing its indoctrination working as insidiously as its most deadly enemy, Communism.

All grey, said Ran. When it isn't whole-hearted black. Miceal liked Ran, a fellow Irishman if a bit difficult to understand, and a rebel against all authority, Churches or fathers.

Look, Miceal. We're really a nation of fighters, OK. And up till a couple of hundred years ago, tribal. We drank and loved and fought without shame.

Artists and poets and fighters, true Celts. We came to this land we love and hate with the sweetness of knives. From the great plains as a great race. With our hounds and our horses and our Great Mother.

We have since been deluded by our leaders, by our Church and by ourselves. Our queens are dead, our goddesses turned into pimply saints, and we have turned our Great Mother of all the earth into an impossible virgin. The Virgin-Mother with her list of don'ts like some bloody landlady. Mother of this, Mother of that, Holy Mother, you never touch your mother and now the message is really home you must never touch any other woman either, for she's now both in your mind.

Jesus, what a lot of impotent, tied-up bastards we are now, the poor bloody Irish.

Ruled by a woman in the wrong way, praying to St. Joseph instead of calling him what he really was, the prize cuckoo of all time and Up the Holy Ghost. Which, as the church would have us believe, is exactly what the clever daw did.

So we drink. O brother, do we drink. To kill despair, pain, betrayal, time and ourselves. It's our way of life. Even the Church can't frown too hard on that. It knows too damn well we'd blow up denied everything else, and half the good Fathers like more than a wee dropeen themselves of Christ's tears. In our dismay we rat out into other countries, and if we stay we say well we can't help being what we are, sure look what Cromwell did to us, and Elizabeth before that, and the Vikings and the Normans and the Milesians and the Firbolgs and Australapithecus and then we were under the sea so bad luck to God.

And we suffer dismal and uproarious and old-fashioned disasters which are no part of the modern world. Others can crash in planes or trains or cars or go under either with dignity and no mess, but we are chopped up by pigs, castrated by bulls, we fall off ladders into barrels of water, we get stuck in bogs and die of O'Rory's Fidgits, we're locked out and die of decent exposure when under the influence of Ma's disapproval, of assaults by hatchet, sure only the little wan, yer Honour, I only used the little wan. The big wan I wouldn't touch at all. I'm illiterate and paralysed and subject to falling down and I'm a decent mon, yer Honour. I had drink taken at the time.

Case dismissed.

And we tear each other to bits with our arms round each other's shoulders. And our Holy Mother eats us. Oink. O we'll fight anyone, yes. If the money's in it.

Still good for a laugh, of course, Old Paddy's a great giggle, the life and soul of the party. No, no, not the Communist party. Never mention that lot at all. The devil himself leads them, he's got one horn already on their hell-red flag. So all together boys, Hail Mary and Dail Eireann. We'll knock shite out of each other and now we've got Telefis Eireann to show us doing it, bedad.

God help us all we say, for nobody else will, the miserable foreign bastards and bad luck in the shape of shamrocks to all of them. Keeping a green bit back of course, for Cromwell.

Restless, faithless, magpie Ran, who was to end his life fighting bitterly as Cuchulain against the rising sea of madness.

Stew would have Miceal down somewhere in a small mental notebook under Primitive.

He had questioned him in the way a fisherman will

carefully turn over a dungheap in search of good worms, transferring thoughts and answers to the baitcan of his mind. He was so interested, so naive in his quest that he seldom offended the most pressed. He asked for outrageous lies, but no-one did so. It was as though he was a big dog that sat on your toe but whose paw you couldn't help taking, Henry had said.

He sat smoking beside Henry, his pleasant open face showing a child's demanding affection for his companions. He smiled a lot and no one had seen him ruffled or angry. Always good-tempered, he patched the others' quarrels, and you couldn't be angry for long with Stew gazing anxiously at you like a dog unfairly scolded.

His eyes gently and lazily missed nothing behind the thick lenses which turned them to raisins. Only when he took his glasses off you found they were large and brown, shrinking again when he put the thick black frames back.

It was a standing joke that his ideal girl must play the harp. At parties he would ask a stranger, Say, that blonde. She wouldn't play the harp by any chance in hell. No I didn't think . . . He'd met two that did, but both were like horses, one in the face and the other built like a quarter-miler, all the muscle in the other end.

The girl with the harp never materialised. Maybe she was only the guardian angel he called upon to hide a tormented heart, for Stew was to die against a hot Morroccan wall, not believing friend death could do this to him, the last cliché. It took him a long time, with jealousy's knife in him and the pretty Arab lad in tears beside him.

Henry, they teased him, talked like a well bred camel. He had a civil, lilting way of speaking, courteous, humourous and with a slow mastery of fencing with words like a rapier, hidden behind a mask of perpetual banter. He was liked by everyone, even those to whom a cultivated voice badgers instantly into snapping like aggressive terriers.

Henry loved roses and impossibly beautiful women. He preferred frank luxury. It never killed anyone, and if it did what a heavenly way of going he said, his long upper lip curving in a dromedary smile. I have the perfect flautist's face. I should have been wedded to my woodwind at an early age. I am filled with lovely intentions towards all. I am absolutely happy with my eccentricities, as God might have said. I have never perverted the cause of justice, dears. Alas, I've never perverted anyone. Which gives one food for thought, and you may all comfort me with Swiss chocolates.

Henry was able to live like a cat in any surroundings, elegant even in complete squalor.

He was to sail effortlessly through medical school before deciding that halitosis, piles and prolapses were part of a humanity he was too sharpened to embrace wholeheartedly. *I don't wish to know that.* Further down the car please, room for one more spastic. Have a hysterectomy this year, and be able to say you've really lived.

Henry was to be a quiet old man, painting alone in a small white house on one side of a Greek island. On the other side of the island, in the only other small white house lived a shepherd and his sheep.

He was still courteous and charming to his sole companion, the long-haired goat Alea. She who grinds he would say, with his curiously sweet smile.

And Paudi. Of whom they said could charm the birds out of the trees. He hadn't long before he was to die. Beside a small fire on the side of an English road, with the cold never to leave his bones and the black tin boiling away into steam. The tin hissed and spat when the water had gone. Between hail showers a missel thrush sang to the shouting blue, until the next storm reared over the hills to drum the fire into flat water, studding it and Paudi's curled body like a nailed boot.

Letty was the only daughter. Her father was a doctor who spent his retirement misjudging the tides of his home creek, so that I'm going for a sail, dear, meant at least four hours dragging himself and his boat across the mud, leaving scored wriggles behind like an injured snail.

Time and tide wait for no man was one of the doctor's favourite sayings, but he had never learned it. He and the village ducks would leave together on the falling tide, waltzing down the narrow channel under the hunched oaks. They would usually spend the day together on the lower reaches of the creek, the ducks swimming tantalisingly in the deep main river only a few yards away, the doctor as high and dry as a stranded whale. In the evening the ducks would swim back again, slapping round him with bright nods to lower into the trickle again and paddle out of sight with the tail of the last drake tight curled as a teacup handle.

As a child Letty had found one of the drakes curled frozen on the lower bank and had picked him up thinking his tail would be still too. She hadn't thought of it as feathers. If you tipped him up he'd pour out she thought, like a jug.

His feet were flat under him like a Chinese carving when you turn it over. She had never forgotten the flat brown parcel body and the eye gone in like a button missing.

You don't want to be stuck away here all your life. You must get out and meet people. The doctor, hauling himself up like a water-rat on the banks, was insistent. Letty had to join sailing clubs and rowing clubs, tennis parties and dramatic societies, all of which involved her in long winding journeys down creeks and up lanes, and in the perennial political arguments of such bodies.

She was perfectly happy to laze around the little village, but her father was determined she should get out and about. See the world. Not vegetate. You're in a rut, Letty, rocking the dinghy like a pig in a muddy trough.

Content to suck and mullet around in his creek, he warned her of Cornwall's diabolical influence, the insidious lichen of destructiveness gnawing into her heart to turn it to stone. As a child she was afraid of the high moors behind the creek, of the wells bubbling darkly of saints and devils, of the stone maidens and frenzied giants. Under her father's goading she professed a deep interest in People, studied social anthropology and found by the time she arrived in Aranchilla that it was only a lead line she swung to get out of her village shoals. Once away and she was out of her depth, no longer captained by her father.

She had loved Melleyn, wondering whether her father was right in his dire beliefs that it choked itself with its own prettiness, gagging in summer on a diet of tourists, and aggravating itself like an ingrowing toenail in winter.

Did it hide something else behind its gingerbread façade, like the Grimms' witch. Her father spoke of ancient tolls taken from Cornwall's human dwellers, its granite heart having extracted everything from the land. Stones split in mad laughter on the heights, and fell on to an earth as acid as when the first rains spat on the hissing sea around it. The humans inherited the nightmares it dreamed through its evolution, its thorns twisted the land and bent themselves. It drowned its fishermen and sailors to the sound of church bells under the sea, mermaids nibbling their hearts away with fishes' needle teeth, it cracked with lightning, flooded mines, made the cuckoo mad as a stone, knocked men and women apart with the strength of feathers.

Every tide laid a treasure of amethysts and bones on a shore fortunate only to the whitened dead. Letty fled.

She adored children, becoming a nanny. All her life was to be with children, though she mothered none of her own.

She and Stew were the only ones in the tent to meet again, when years later she was with a family in Egypt.

He stood on the burning step in the heat, someone else behind him. She couldn't see.

O Stew. How *lovely* to see you. *My dear*.

She went to kiss him and he drew back. He wasn't smiling. I heard you were here, he said.

He looked ill. He didn't introduce the shadow behind him, she could see it was a boy in a fez. They stood like husband and wife calling, the husband the old friend.

He seemed unable to say anything, and went away quickly. She hadn't said goodbye.

She felt shocked, as though she had touched a ghost and felt nothing. She wondered afterwards whether he was not already dead, peeling his shadow off the white wall like someone ripping bark from a tree.

As an old woman she returned to Cornwall, old

104

enough to be now untroubled by her father's ghost, and by the old things of an old land.

Old enough to draw near to the small stone house which finally encloses all travellers in the tin kingdom, without fear of past ghosts or of those to come.

Britt talked of her childhood in Sweden, where her father's estate with its pleasant meadows and streams bordered the forest, which was a mysterious dark land to the children, where anything could happen. They were forbidden to go into it alone as there were lynx still in the deepest parts. Sometimes you saw the stern-eyed eagle owls who looked as though they had once been philosophers, now turned into feathers by a forest magician. And they were taken on elk hunts, running all day with the bush-tailed grizzled Spitz hounds which looked like wolves. Britt hated it when they brought one to bay, the silence hanging like a curtain from the pine branches splintered by the shrill explosions of the barking hounds. The great elk wasn't noble in death somehow, like a stag. Bigger, but ridiculous with those big Jewish candlesticks on his head, his muffin bell dangling, his lugubrious trombone face and his oversize goloshes. You couldn't feel suitably sad when he lay there with the expression of one to whom everything happens, and this beats all.

It was funny to see one rise suddenly out of the lake, the weed hanging from its antlers like the Keystone Cops' car rushing out of some predicament with them all hanging on at the sides. It was only if you were lucky enough to see one running through the forest that you took it all back. The shafts of sunlight spearing his eye, bending his body as big as a boat through the battalions of pines like a fish through weeds, and manoeuvering his great antlers like a dexterous waiter with a high hand of plates.

Winter, with the white presence behind the snow, some-one or something which strides behind the curtain, when the forest moved in behind you when you weren't looking, like Grandmother's Footsteps. You had to keep looking round, suddenly, to keep it back, afraid it would leap on you with a whacking of icy branches, hooting, lynx-clawed. With the fox writing his diary on the white days and nights, the red spots of some small death on the counterpane of the meadows, and the swans calling you away with them to their kingdom of heartbreak, whistling over the bald iced pate of the lake with its faded grasses and rushes sticking up like fair hairs.

To summer, when the forest went back again behind the wooden fences, and lay down humming in the heat and shimmering with boilings of gnats.

And you rode on your yellow pony, with the white Swedish mane like your own hair, with the tall grass parting over his knees, dusting them and your tickled feet with pollen, and the storks that came every year standing around on their roof nests like castaways in anchored barrels.

They clattered their beaks as though praying to each other up there in their spindly mosques, like muezzins accompanying themselves with the flamenco levity of castanets.

And the butter from the red and white cows was golden, your skin dusted golden with the sun and bathing in the lakes, as though summer had rubbed

106

against you like a great golden cat, and the summer moon that ballooned over the forest as though she'd never get up high enough to clear the puncturing pine tops, and would come rolling and bumping down over the meadows until the red barn stopped her.

And the sky so blue it made you gasp and ache with it being so far up there, so blue it passed God. No wonder the Swedish flag was blue and gold. But somewhere there should be white for winter too. To be chosen Queen of Light was to bring summer and winter together, the white snow dress and the golden sun candles, and all the fiddles creaking away like the ice squeaking at the spring thaw.

Like the embroidered jacket to be worn until you were too hot or too cold and had to take it off. Red and orange, blue and yellow, white flowers stitched with green button-holes down the front.

The rejoicing cranes slipping green crowns over the heads of birches as they left their arrow trails for spring to follow, and death one white swan with no reflection on a black lake.

Britt was so happy telling them, radiating her happiness among them that none could feel untouched by its glow.

She was to brush all she met with the moth quality of this happiness, and her children later.

Britt's life was not to be, as are some lives, predictable by the plan or pattern inherent in them, a pattern chosen by them or which chooses them, queen or pawn.

Britt was to have nothing defined, so many decisions and possibilities, the difficult and lonely paths of one who thinks and feels deeply, and for whom nothing is

107

trivial. Few achieve the completeness and acceptance which, without fear, she would take with her on her journey.

All she would carry was a face beautiful even in extreme age, the white hair of her youth becoming whiter with years, and a light which burned as brightly as the crown of candles when she was Queen of Light one winter's day.

You look just like a peppermint angel, sweetie, Henry said when she stopped suddenly, afraid she had bored them, and shy.

They had rigged a green storm sheet over the tent, and the light through the walls turned her fair hair and pale dress into an unearthly translucent green, as though she was sitting under the sea.

Have a green jelly-baby. Henry handed her a battered paper bag. You look like God's gift to Lorca at the moment, hon. How much I want you green. And behold she is. The little genius.

Selene was to take the place of the son they wanted.

Always it had been you should have been a boy, until one day in her efforts to run, ride, swim or fight better than any boy, she cut off her hair and had to have the mess that was left cut even closer to get it growing evenly again. The professor had not objected to her adoption and had thought her a charming little creature, wild as a goat's kid. Yes yes, of course Adele, do what you feel is best. Poor little mite. And how amazing, my dear, quite amazing to be found abandoned on the mountain like some young immortal; a young goddess.

One hot day her village had tilted and poured its houses and its peasants into the smoking mouth of the

108

earth. The small girl, a boy and a big white shepherd's dog were found together in the ruined temple of Selene, high on the mountainside above the village. The dog had lost his master and his flock, and had attached himself zealously to the two children, shepherding them out of the dust and up to the cool rocks where there was a spring of water. The boy was carried out of Selene's life wrapped in a blanket, and the professor saw only a grave, dishevelled child fostered remarkably by a large dog as Zeus by his goat, or those others left by fate or intention to become immortals among men and gods.

The small Selene wept bitterly as her shaggy defender was beaten away to follow anxiously from a distance as she was taken through the big grey iron gates of the professor's garden. They were locked with a clang, and the dog came up to the bars and put his nose through them sadly. Then he sat with his back pressed tightly against them and sighed and dozed in the heat. When night came he curled up like a rolled rug, occasionally twitching his nose and whiskers, his black bear's eyes flickering open with the matt stare of unseeing.

Selene was uncontrollable at first, which they thought was shock. But at the first chance she ran down through the garden and along the high walls where the olive trees leaned like old men on sticks, to the gates where the big dog still waited. Sneezing happily he grinned and wriggled, itching with delight and relief, one hind leg scratching emptily at his sagging back. He licked the small brown hands held out to him through the railings, and at every opportunity Selene stole food for him, scraping it off the plates and burying them afterwards. He ate everything she brought him, rich and unsuitable so that he itched worse and erupted with

garlic belches. For her he was the only safe thing left
before and after the time when the earth had warned
her it was going to roar like a bull and gore her village
into dust. The dog had also known it, and the donkeys
which brayed and hiccoughed and were beaten for
being more contrary than ever. The silly, spectacled
donkeys, for no one heeds the drunken man when he
cries Wolf.

Selene was so badly shocked by the loss of her
mother and one brother, that the past was blocked for
her into the one stream of Now, and the dog. Her
father had died before she could remember him, in
one of the chaotic thunder storms of the mountains,
running with his goats to shelter in one of the caves
above the temple of Selene. To her, Father meant little.
Sometimes he was a man, sometimes the wind or the
leaves, the electric lizard or the first drops of the storm
which run through the groves like silk. So much had
gone from her and the small boy gone too, but the dog
remained. The dog and she had survived the end of
their world.

Selene was caught by one of the gardeners. She had
walked past him unnaturally stiff and bulky and he had
followed her quietly. When she came to the gates she
had pulled out a long loaf from the front of her dress,
and unloaded a surprising array of packages from her
knickers. Like a squirrel she buried two plates from
the mixture, and turned to run when she saw him
watching. Fear, rage and guilt made her sick on the
spot. So intense were her pleadings that the household
feared for her reason, and they decided to let in the
big dog. He could live in the stables after he'd been

110

thoroughly bathed by the under-gardener. The dog accepted everything calmly, and gradually he was no longer tied up, but padded around the garden and into the house as he wished.

They took off the thick leather collar with the iron spikes against the wolves of the mountain, and one of the grooms made him a special one engraved with the name they gave him, Crotopus — The Thumper. For Selene he took the place of her lost brother and, the human mind being a strange confection, when in years to come the word brother was mentioned Selene saw the thick, white curls and black Chinese eyes of Crotopus. When he had become very old and slow, one night he climbed the stairs heavily and went quietly into Selene's room, looking down into her sleeping face. He knew he was forbidden upstairs, but he also knew this time they wouldn't mind. He curled up at the side of her bed, sighed, and dreamed that he was dead.

They buried him beside the iron gates, so that he could look in or out as he wished, and one of the gardeners took a donkey and cart and brought back a fallen slab from the temple where he and Selene had been found. On it they carved Crotopus, The Dog.

Selene was given a black running hound, but for her there would always be just the one dog, white and curly as the lambs he was bred to guard, and big enough in the heart to stand against the wolf or the world.

Selene's foster father, the professor, lived in the past; he saw everyone as a god or a mortal. There were few gods, he found. He named Selene carefully, and he felt fortunately. He brought her up on a rich diet of omens, classics, portents and Voices from Olympus. He was not interested in her as a child, nor later as an individual, but as a new receptacle for his obsession, a fresh ear to hear the gods again through his intercession and translation. For her, he was as remote as Zeus and far less interesting.

One day she found her real father. O she had thought, this is my father, this is surely my father. He is not the rain, nor the leaves nor the wind, but this beautiful creature who loves me as I give him my love. Glistening black, chained to each side of his stall, with shining half-moons eclipsing the round darkness of his eyes when he turned to watch her. Gentle and powerful, the silken Spanish stallion listened with his curved, quick ear to all she told him, and breathed warmly down on to her small head, twiddling affectionately at her ribbon with his cushioned upper lip.

It was unusual to keep horses in Greece, but Professor Christoforu liked to think of himself as the ideal European country gentleman, for him a mixture of Xenephon, the Georgics and an Edwardian English squire. The horses, 'My Thessalian Mares' to the professor despite their sex, and the two Spanish stallions, Bienmirado and Pegaso, were kept mainly for visiting friends to enjoy, as the professor found, however ardently he admired them, he was no Alexander when it came to riding them. The Spanish grooms devotedly tended them, waxing and plumping them in the manner of grooms everywhere, and becoming sparse and brittle themselves as though all their being was poured into the shining moulds of their charges, leaving them only wrinkled skins on a pithed frame, eyes like pips and pitted with acid when their darlings were taken out by strangers, their great children taken away from their silent, impotent criticism by fools.

Dogs were the same. They were all Molassian

112

Hounds, and the professor, a modern Acteon, sped
happily along the curved shores of the bay below his
home calling in hunting tones to a varied assortment of
greyhounds, pointers, great danes and bloodhounds, to
Bronte and Laelaps, Aethon, Lampos and Argus, and
hoping he would run into Artemis round the next
headland. It had occurred to him that he would have a
hard time controlling his motley pack if she was in her
usual disguise of a deer, and no woman, other than
Aphrodite of course, could turn as nasty in so short a
time ... Heel, Apollo. Good girl, Demeter, there's my
sweet girl. Leave it, Leander, dirty dog. *Leave* it, I say.
O you despicable hound.

🐎

His wife, a saddened little French woman, had been so
many things immortal and mortal, that she could no
longer keep a count of them. She had at various times
been Aphrodite and Hera, Hecate and Sycorax, girl
and crone, head of barley. And Black Sow when things
went wrong. She felt by now she had three heads,
whined softly and kept out of the way of her bossy little
Zeus. The professor, whose amorous propensities suffered dismally from a total lack of accepting reality,
longed to complete his pursuits by sudden transforma-
tions into horses, clouds, bulls and the rest of that
zoological collection which brought mythological suc-
cess to the Father of the Gods in interesting situations.
  Adele was now so ineffective and subdued that
Selene found early she needed no substitute mother.
Kept away from the servants, among whom she might
have found a human anchor, with only the big sleepy
bitches as sisters and aunts, the one small Arab mare
in the stables became mother enough, and even then
Selene had to accept her rejection when she foaled.

As she grew, all her adventures were taken on horseback, all the decisions and emergencies and dangers which horses bring, situations needing quickness of thought and action, truths which she need never know in the scented safety of the statuesque garden. Her small graceful frame concealed an unexpectedly wiry strength, a quiet sureness emanated from her in the presence of horses, and a frightening adult wisdom which left her a child still when she was away from them. On a horse, a strange intensity burned, carving her serious little face into a dark and inturned mask, and they went proudly for her as for no one else. She helped the grooms to break and train them, knowing better than they did how to turn a horse's great strength against himself, like water. To her a horse was like the sea and the land. Neither yields yet both give. And the true control, the thin thread not of traditional silk but of concentration and will, of spirit and spirit. A horse alive, unhumbled, and the classic rider who needs no thought, but is.

The grooms worshipped her with an old faith, and she was to find men easier to break than horses; the same sugary promise held out to both, the halter hidden behind the back. And both will take the curb if it is first sweetened.

Selene was happiest when riding along the sands where dolphins rode beside her at sea, the Andalusian arching and stepping, profoundly attentive to her wishes and contented in himself.

They would both eye the black rock ahead, where Selene felt this would be the place should the Bull ever come again out of the sea. Once she found a strange track and hoofmarks, and the rock like the black bull waiting.

She followed the marks to the next village up the

114

bay, and, half relieved, discovered they were made by an olive tree washed up and dragged away by mules for firewood.

Hippolytus had been a fool, you should never wind anything round your hand with horses, it was asking for trouble. And he would probably have had his reins around his wrist. A good horseman would check his harness first, and surely the chariot's ring-pin too. She felt no pity for him, only the exasperation of a goddess.

Funny how you can't laugh when you have an obsession, which can also be the Achille's tendon of the obsessed, she realised years later.

Dear old Crotopus, and yet I wasn't really adopted by him. I wouldn't have liked an eagle or a goat or a wolf, though, like those others. A horse, yes. Pegasus and Helicon on a hot day like this. All those tiresome muses languishing around, they'd have to find somewhere else to go. And even with Wisdom's golden bridle, all those who had actually ridden Pegasus had come to grief, the incompetent fools. On the Andalusian's black shoulder she traced where the wings would be. Yes, it would be different. You'd have to sit far back and risk sliding off as he would have the softest of mouths, or you might be able to sit nearer the withers and keep your feet forward so as not to interfere with him taking off. She bent and laid her cheek against the silky cascade of the Spanish stallion's mane. How lovely horses smell in the heat.

Or I would have chosen Cheiron, the centaur.

Many years and many tears later Selene was to cry bitterly. Never, never lay the heavy mantle of a goddess's name on a mortal, who must die. You may fasten it with the glittering pin of destruction, for you bear the double guilt of the immortals, and the immortal guilt of mortals who die in you, wishing it. Or you the sacrifice for them.

And if any man force you to turn against your *geasa* you have to die. Die in the heart before the time of the phoenix can come, and sometimes it cannot, and there is only the flame. Selene's *geasa* was her power over horses, and the power they had over her. Love was one man who was to enter the magic circle they lunged around her, a Perseus who held up the mirror not to blind her but to show her she wore the double mask of Demeter the Fury, and as she fell near madness brought her Pegasus, ready bridled. And she now had the wisdom not to wish to ride him.

Selene learned early and learned secretly in the stables and in the groves, of love. Her body was part of the earth and of the days and nights, and she used its power savagely. *I love you. O, I love you.* Love me and hate me, for I reject both. Men were drowned in her terrible innocence, the innocence of the goddess who must die in the struggle for immortality. To lose the insanity of innocence, to leave the double-headed guardianship of the Bull or Goat, Wolf or Eagle or Horse.

To turn innocence into wisdom by an alchemy of the spirit which is the true immortality.

Selene knew she could not remain with the Christoforus; the princess locked in the enchanted garden of forever. In the day the garden became so intensely embalmed in the drugging and overpowering scents of roses and wistaria, lemon and orange flowers, that it was like a funeral for summer, rigid under the heat and weight of its own flowers. It held a dreadful, dreamlike quality as though it masked a worming sea of decay, the nightingales hammering out the mazes with metallic insistency, nailing the stones to the paths, and the cypresses sticking up like big ones they couldn't drive in, black splinters pegging their roots down among the urns like crucified hands. In the waiting before thunder you could her the dolphins gasp and pump in the bay below, and the olive trees came forward suddenly threatening, epileptics frozen with clawing arms, prisoners stretched on their twisted trunk racks, but the thunder always got to them before they could cry out or curse.

At night the garden was thickly sugared by moonlight, drenched in scents as though bottles of stars had been sprinkled over it in hundreds and thousands, and the nightingales iced it into fantastic designs which deafened it as they hardened.

Selene knew if she stayed she would be trapped like a bee in the window of an empty house, brittle and mummified like the digested fly in the heart of the carnivorous flower.

It wasn't that she had no fondness for them, the Professor and his wife. She was deeply grateful, which only made it worse, yet desperately aware she must get out of the beautiful cage to fly alone, with no hurt surprise

117

and recriminations, the tedious cud swallowed and re-swallowed of where we went wrong, and you.

She went before the dawn, when the rusty-sawing donkeys began to creak and push through the gap that fences night from day, before the cockerels pricked each house into life with a pin of light, the villages stitched themselves among the rocks with threaded candles, and the hills wandered back from the darkness like grazing beasts.

She travelled first to Florence, to stay with an uncle. A city she had always loved on previous visits with the professor, but now she found the greatness of the past top heavy, the buildings shouldering over to crush her, the blank stares of people and statues, the insistent neurotic strutting of the pigeons, and the shrill evening attack on the squares by the knifing swallows strangely disturbing.

She felt out of time, incongruous as a dry leaf left from autumn to blow in the spring winds among the coming green; brittle and sharp, unwanted by memory or reason. The fountains drummed like fingers playing on a nerve, the male pigeons around her sandals throt-tled and pumped with little, hard eyes after the smoothly evading hens, palsied with desire on patting, irregular coral feet. Their bridling rainbow necks caught the light like the nacreous interior of shells. They traced stutter-ing clockwork patterns like toys, yes yes nodding. One bathed messily with beating wings like someone hitting at flies with a newspaper. It shook itself in the air and a drop of water fell on her hand. *Dear Father, Dear Mother, I am sorry.* Always you were sorry.

It was May. She thought of the Camargue and the big Provençal farm house of one of the French Christoforus, who had been as successful a sire as any one of his selected bulls. His large family had encompassed the dark girl of the uncanny gift with horses as just another creature among the animal and child population of the Mas d'Isle.

On her visits to them with the Professor, she became a talisman, a harbinger of fortune to the herds, and the taciturn Guardians had the same profound respect and affection for her as the Professor's grooms. The grave child would be given the tall white Syrian, and flanked by the Guardians, ride out to the black herds as ceremoniously as the Queen of Sheba with her attendants.

All the visiting Spanish cuadrillos stayed at the Mas d'Isle when corridas were held in Nîmes and Arles, and Jean Christoforu, as well as breeding the wide-horned French fighting bulls, also trained horses for both French and Spanish rejoneadores.

Selene was adored by them all, from the crabbed swordhandlers to the successful matadors, and rode the highly trained rejoneo stallions with such poise and élan that the horsemen talked of her becoming another Citron. But the Professor had always whisked her away.

A strange thing had happened in the great arena at Arles, during one of the Spanish corridas, and which was already a Camargue legend. The last bull of the afternoon was behind the toril, the entire will of the large audience pinned to the red door behind which he waited in the warm darkness for his second and more terrible birth into the light. Selene had been taken down into the callejon, completely against the regulations, to watch the last faena from the comparative safety near the big doors of the entrance. The head

119

herdsman from the ranch which supplied the bulls held
her up so that she could see over the top boarding, but
ready for immediate retreat in case the bull should
jump the barrera. The toril gates swung open, but the
darkness was complete. Sometimes they walked out
nervously as stags, sometimes they trotted with high
heads and loosely swinging tails like hackneys into a
showring, sometimes they came out roaring like trains
from a tunnel. This one, nothing. It was as though the
darkness in there hadn't finished making a bull. Then
he was out, the dark square of the toril fell back behind
him like a portcullis, and he carried all its gathered
blackness with him straight into the middle circle of
the arena, where he stood watching, pivoting quickly
with his scorpion head flashing, like a black fly on a
handless clock face.

He flew at the first cape, scissoring with head and
feet, a low rumbling mixed with a stringy froth from
his half-open mouth, splintering one horn into a
chrysanthemum on the boards of the burladero. He was
a classic bull, smooth as a train, on rails, like silk. He
insisted under the pic. All the clichés were applied to
him like price-tags pinned on to his heaving, pumping
scarred hide.

The trumpets sounded for the last faena, he was to
be dedicated to an actress, stony behind her dark
glasses, smiling redly, hands elaborately graceful.

The bull had stopped near the barrera and the
perched Selene. He would not leave his querencia and
Orthella had to work him there. At the last pass he
crossed one foot and fell onto his knees. Wearily he
got up and walked away from Ortella to the barrera
below Selene who craned to see him, now wrecked and
unsteady, his hump castrated with pain and loss of
blood into a flat cow's neck, his eyes going into shadow.

The crowd were uneasy, Manolete had gone the same way, with the bull dangerously defending, without impulsion. Ah-hé-heh. Toro. Ehé, toro. Ortella did not command, there was compassion in his call. The bull hung his gaze on the bright figure, then looked up and turning to the barrera he walked quietly up to where Selene suddenly leaned forward over it from the herdsman's shoulders, and to his horror, stretched out her hand. From the flaring seats there was a deep gasp like pine trees sighing. Before there was time to snatch her away, the bull reached up to it and licked it, and she saw him shaking with the effort, his straining eyes rolling back like marbles at their pocket corners. It was one of those odd moments from an animal still dangerous, a slip of attention, inattention or a reflex. And yet perhaps, as the minds of animals are still unknown, intended. It lasted a moment. Selene knew when it would end, and Ortella and the herdsman. She drew back her hand and the bull waited, heaving. Ortella turned and asked permission to dedicate. Instead of the actress he came back to the barrera and dedicated the bull to Selene. There was a roar of applause, and Selene cried out involuntarily No, oh no. Don't kill him. Then she straightened. She accepted the bull with grave dignity and bowed to Ortella. As the sword entered she felt the pain herself. Slowly like a tent collapsing, his hind quarters sagged and he sat looking like a big horned dog and ridiculous. *Die, O die bull,* she begged silently. The sword stuck out of his shoulders like a tea-cup handle from the thick blood which guttered down both forelegs as though from melting red candles and the frilled bandilleras clattering like bamboos in a wind.

He threw his head back and fell on his side, one hind leg twitching. One of the cuadrillos worked the

121

puntilla in well and the dull head rattled its teeth. The leg stopped twitching. Ortella carried her round the ring on his shoulders, and she would always remember the hard, sharp edges of his sequined jacket, the smell of brilliantine and sweat and the blood on the hand holding her feet.

Mon cher Oncle ...

Of course you must come, but naturally. We are again en fête, and the Gitanes have been here already nearly a fortnight. Al Borak is getting whiter and older like myself, but we have a new pure Andalusian for you of curious colouring, very like a Velasquez. He comes on well, the young Salud, and would make you a charming companion for your stay. As long as you wish dear daughter, forever if it is necessary. Devotedly.

Jean met her at the station, and they drove under the bridge and past the Hotel Van Gogh, where her uncle took off his hat in salute, and as usual nearly crashed the old Peugeot round the corner. They honked through the market stalls and people shouted and waved to them from pavements piled with vegetables and cow bells, lamps and beads, resigned fowl, knickers and matronly rabbits, hats and a tail-less peacock on a string. They had to slow down at the traffic lights, and as always Selene looked into the blacksmith's cavern, precariously edged between the houses and traffic like someone trying not to step into the road, and liable you felt to receive a berserk taxi into its dark mouth rather than the big Percherons and Belgians that came there. A glimpse of the great ink-blotched Dane lying on his side in the cool entrance, big bronze hams and flaxen tail and the smith working on a foot, the horse

122

shining out of the darkness the way horses do, as though the smith had just cast one for himself, and was now smoothing over the rough joins with his file and would soon burnish the whole, the bronze horse turning into gold as it came out into the sun.

Out in the country, the bamboos rustled beside the narrow road, parting and closing again as though something was pushing through them. Selene as a child had expected to see a lion coming out, his yellow eyes half-closed against the tickling shoots, to jump over the dykes and pud down the road. She used to imagine him arriving at the sea, nose and tail gently switching, leaving great jellymould foot marks on the blinding sands. One of the Algerian gypsies might be sleeping it off, and the lion would be too hot and amazed to do anything but sniff and then walk away, or even lie down beside him. Was the Douanier so wrong, she thought now as the country opened like a panting dog's mouth with spiky teeth bushes and white egrets caught like feathers on thorns. The land creaked with heat and frogs.

Funny what some paintings did. There was the small graveyard, high white walls and the enclosed dead done to a blue cinder. Here, with the smell of wax and sweetness and glass humming, the iron bars striping the graves and the zebra picking his way through the monuments with the tight coquetry of lifted hooves and grid-iron head cocked to the ground as though listening for the dead to rattle drily. The parachute might land on the zebra, and then look out, or engulf the commiserating Virgin who leaned over M. Latouche and gave him the password to heaven. Or it might float down outside, and when you rushed out there was nothing there. Only the frogs and the zebra barking. And who was on the end of it. And God the Father

123

sent his only begotten son. The zebra had eaten all the flowers, even the wax ones. He stood at the gates, nodding briskly with his Parthenon mane shaking, his eyes like grapes, flapping his ears with the black ranula tips. Ha-ha, quha-ha, surely they meant a zebra among the trumpets. Now he had eaten the sun, and bits of it stuck on his long yellow teeth like fried egg. Selene woke as the Peugeot, like a whirlgig beetle, shot into the long drive with its rows of ceremonial umbrella pines squatting on their mushroom shadows.

The white-washed Mas d'Isle, with its carp-scale roof and heavy grey shutters was quiet in the last of the heat. Jean and Selene sat silently for a moment, and she looked up at the rows of geraniums in the antique pots on the steps, and the wall of the thatched stables which was a curious not-white, not just from the arsenic sprayed on the vines trained against it, but as though someone had thought green into the brush. Behind was a kraal of thatched cabins crouching in its lea away from the wind-claws of the lion mistral. Somewhere a horse was being put round, a quick soft thudding in the sand, the sharp blowing and sneezing of a horse well in himself yet attending, the spark of a bit and the creaking of leather. A quiet whistling, and the occasional low word. Jean smiled at Selene. Welcome. Always. Soon she would be flooded by the laughter and greetings, barked at and jumped on, taken to see the new kittens, the new pups, the new chicks, alas, who had died since she left, yes old Poseidon was still throwing the bravest bulls in the whole of France, and O Selene we have a new stallion from Jerez.

She took out the white-splashed mahogany Salud,

but he was young and exaggerated, and bounced, his
four feet charlestoned and flashed and he enjoyed parad-
ing through the crowded village, eyeing the shop
windows and shaking foam over everyone. One of the
gypsies had given her a half-moon brooch of pearls,
and she wore it in her hair. Selene, La Déesse. Comme
elle est belle. Ca va, Petite. They called to her and she
had to visit them and drink strawberry tea, dance for
them, sing for them. Last time she had loved Java by
night on the cool sands. He had wanted to marry her.
A great celebration and much fortune at Sara's festival.
Now he came with her into the crypt and lit a candle
for them both. But he looked at Selene, not at Sara.
He took her by the shoulders as they climbed back up
the dark steps, fumbling in the darkness, and pressed
her against the cold crypt wall as he kissed her. She
laughed and bit him in the neck hard. A group of long-
skirted girls came down, their Coptic eyes glittering in
the light from the massed candles. Java's eyes were
yellow like a big cat. She knew it couldn't last, she
could never be the wife Java wanted. Soon the heat
would go, and the fighting and drinking and servitude
begin. *Chovahauni* he said, his tiger's face hard in the
sun. They went back together to the big black tent,
where Salud was held by an admiring group of young
boys, very high headed, looking down his long Spanish
nose and starting occasionally at the noise and con-
fusion with feet clattering like castanets. Someone was
playing a guitar to him, and the base of his ears was
black with sweat under the bridle. He was beginning to
strike out and rear, scaring his circling attendants when
Selene came back. She hitched up her long skirt and
jumped up on him, kicking with her bare feet until Java
gave her a lift. He held onto her bare knee. There was
laughter and shouted obsenities. She pressed Salud and

he crouched, then rose into a controlled lévade like a big wave calmly out of the sea. Java stepped back. Then the stallion walked forward on his hind legs, his forelegs beating until she dropped him and let him go, and he flung out his feet, curving and bending himself like a flag flying in honour of his young rider. Small boys sped after him, and the gypsies cheered and waved as the shining horse flashed past them and out onto the dunes where he crested along their ridges like a brown dolphin, glad to be away from the crowds, gritting on his bit and blowing and fluttering down his nostrils.

In one of the hollows she nearly ran down a small shabby tent and the astonished Henry and Stew, who were beginning supper on a driftwood fire. The next day she came back to apologise, leaving the impetuous Salud behind and riding a small white Camarguais, who would wait quietly for as long as she wished, and who would not foam over everyone and tango around unsociably. Several days later she decided to join Henry and Stew camping up through France where Ran was to meet them in Paris, and where they all hoped to share their remaining money to get them to Ireland. She sat by their fire and drank bad tea. She was not worried where they went. Jean had sighed. We cannot keep you, ma chère. Only God can do that. I shall always come back, you know that. Dear Jean and Maman.

To where the bull threads the black needles of land into the quilted sea and the white horses carry the salt bloodline of Ocean, by Time out of Legend.

126

They met Letty and Britt in the Dordogne. The two girls had set up their tent in a sheltered valley by the Vezére, and Britt had looked up from the primus as they had walked past in the shadows of the road. The sun caught Britt's hair as she had turned, and Letty waved. Why don't you join us, there's no one else here now. They saw the two tall young men consult the dark girl with them who looked like a Tahitian or a gypsy.

Ah good, said Selene. That night she moved into the girls' new blue and yellow tent, not because she was worried over moral appearances but because their's was bigger and Stew snored. She would burrow against Henry's long side, for once asleep he never moved, flat on his back like a stone Crusader, his lined face white as alabaster, but the sound wedged past all defences.

They decided they'd all go on to Paris, and the girls said once there and they would think about Ireland. They went by bus for the last part of the journey, and Henry said O Lord it's far too hot to be sweltering in Paris. Let's get off at Chartres. Ran can get a train down. We'll wire him.

They camped under the poplars by the little black stream. Behind them in a small sunlit field of childhood's everlasting daisies and buttercups, five black and white cows lay in the shadows and became black and blue. In the evening they all got up and shouldered quietly out into the warmth to graze, joined by a massive fawn battleship of a bull with Assyrian curls down his face and dewlaps hanging like blankets on a washing line.

O God. Selene had prayed. *Make me a better person. O God let me see.* She was blind with tears.

The great stones reared up from man's profoundest foundations of longing to his most triumphant transcendental vision, crowned with the sun and the moon, God and Lucifer.

They came down the steps into the square where the sun hit them like balls against a wall, and they staggered with heads ringing with red and blue, inarticulate with singing, stunned with understanding.

Ran was waiting for them. He had bought a small embroidered velvet cap from a stall near the cathedral. Hello there he said, and put it on Selene's head. Good luck, Juliet. Yours ever, Romeo.

They sat up by the fire when the others had gone to bed, and a nightingale flung his saeta from the willows. The cows tufted and sighed and thumped down to doze as the chimes chained the hours. They went into the field. Mind the cow-pats. I'm more worried about that bull. He won't hurt you, not while I'm here. He wouldn't anyway. The hours when even night curls to sleep between bells. You're a strange creature, Selene. And you, Ran. I am that.

In the morning they looked at each other, and the others knew. She and Ran went together like uncoupled hounds, close, yet free to break. Ran didn't ask her of love, or demand it. He laughed and loved quickly and angrily like an animal. He didn't question or probe, cutting out pieces of Before and After, and trying to stick them together again.

A child and a woman, Selene knew too little and too much. Her instinctive animal patience, an awaiting to allow the patterns of life to form and change, were to bring her wisdom, but only when she ceased to fight the water and the rock.

They were watching a bubbling tank with big Seurat trout in the window of a restaurant. It's a hell of a long way to Tipperary said Ran. Is everyone game. Any more for the bog.

A sad El Greco waiter peered at them. Ca va, Sebastian. Had any good arrows lately. Henry smiled and bowed, and the El Greco returned bleakly into his martyrdom of bunions and escargots, and Mon Dieu les Anglais. Oui Madame, they are truly the legs of the frog. No Madame, I do not know how they were despatched. Yes, Madame, they are truly snails. Absolutely. O an unspeakable dose of the green pox to Madame. *Fernand*. Oui, Monsieur. Un moment ...

They sat at a mosaic table on rubber-tipped chairs that mooed when moved, and counted among deux bières, un café noir and trois cafés au lait their combined resources and expectancies. Well you women, how about it. We'll come said Selene. Dear God, the touching eagerness of the young said Ran, squinting like a bull terrier over the big green cup. Yez'll all die roaring.

Going back to the tents they crossed the road by the shop under the gilded horse's head which to Selene looked about to cry out like the prince in the fairytale.

A large blue dish with an array of elegant pink joints and rolls among the parsley was labelled in large black writing Special for This Week, Foal. They had to drag her past, speechless with rage and condemnation. But Lenie, we all eat calves. It's the same thing. She flew at Henry, dancing like a run-over cat. How *could* you say that. I could *kill* you. O I could *kill* them in there. How *could* you even think of it, a foal, *a foal*. God the bad luck, the *hate* I wish on them all back there. It's like murder. If you could kill a foal you could kill *anyone*.

How shall we do it. Let's see, now. If Monsieur cuts his finger he could die of the Strangulating Hockbite and Madame on her way to confession could be satisfactorily ground to pulp under a dray of runaway Percherons, and if she had a horse-drawn funeral they'll shit all the way to the church and eat her wreaths. Satisfied. Can you think of anything else. She had to laugh. But it's such a lovely Arab head. I wish they wouldn't make it so *beautiful*.

The first darts of rain hit the tents and she knew that Miceal wanted her. This was a time when she must take no bridle, when the gate must be closed so quietly that he would not know he was enclosed. Miceal saw her watching him. He felt dry in the mouth, tight across the face and eyes. He got up quickly and pushed out. Well, I'll be heading off. There's a power of wind to come. Paudi examined the ropes and tested the pegs. He shrugged, his hands in his pockets. I'll be on up later. He turned and faced the hard wind off the sea, his black hair flagging with the gusts. Will you be down tomorrow Mike, that is if we're still all in one piece. Miceal thought of the croft. Hell, no. There was more shelter by the lake, it was for them to decide. Aye, I might. I'll see ye sometime for I'm away up to Coolnay with the sheep all the morning. He knew Selene had heard.

There was old spotted-arse and his clan tucked under the dancehall for the blow. Funny how even a new one had the sense to find the best place. Better even than the tinkers. Spot, ye'll need it surely this night. The

130

island reeled under the fists of the wind which battered it not with a steady force but with squalling, black punches. Rain gobbed down here and there in big splats as though marking out a target, and then as he ran the last yards up to the cabin, it lifted a solid curtain of water and threw it over Aranchilla like someone throwing a bucket over a sleeping pig.

Holy Mother who knows so much. Help me for I'm destroyed in the heart. Tell me is it love to be like this. That measures me on my days like the shadow on the mountain. Mother of God I am marked by it as the ram marks the ewe with his painted breast. No, that's an unholy thought but you know surely what I mean is the truth. Pray for me, Holy Mother, a sinner and unworthy. Mother of God help me. The grey fox twisting in the steel, your son Jesus, pray for me. Love is a word. Only. For angels and the Holy. Thou shalt love thy God. Love me, Baby, yeah yeah. Verily I say. And God so loved the world. Begotten, forgotten. Amen. The grey fox litters her quick and bitter love in the rocks. Blessed is the fruit of thy womb. Mary the fox, pray for me. He looked up over his hands.

She blessed him with her chief-guide's salute. Sea damp had leprosied her pink cheeks, a knock chalked her nose like a dart score. Two fingers off like Micky Docherty in the timber saw. Our Lady of Perpetual Suckers. Succour the wee sucking pig. Jesus, the great tits on her, gran's prize Ulster. Fourteen and all going strong as a brewery. Will ye listen to the hail. Hail Mary, full of grace. I must be going now, and ending. Will ye be putting the three pennies in now, Miceal. Take a hold of button B and try again. For the dead

131

man's eyes. One a penny, two a penny, hot Christ bun.
If ye haven't a penny a halfpenny will do, God bless
ye Child. The powers of love, the Jamesons, the Holy
Souls, St. Patrick three goals and Croagh Patrick
Park. Up the Holy Ghost. Amen.

The storm was over by morning. In the sudden ways
of the island the sky was bell clear and chiming with
light. Spinning clear for miles and sparkling, the silence
so bright and flashing it turned the mind into quartz,
cutting away bone and carpeting hair to the encased
bedrock skull ringing crystal. Until light and sound
rang together, tingling and fizzling along the pointing
grasses up the deaf stone mountain and off into the
cloud cap which was whipped into blue and thrown
away. Voices and bells circled up in the ringing goblet
of air like hawks winding, dogs' glass barks flew and
splintered like minnows, a cow horned the sun up like
an orange. Cocks crew together, then raggedly like
bellringers missing a pull, and each ass blew down his
own Jericho around the cabin walls. Pigs bassooned in
potato soup, the first bees twanged by on fiddlers'
wings. Far away to the smaller lake, where the mizzen
star and his herd humped like whales through the sea
of bushes, the butter-fingered bittern dropped his
euphonium at intervals. He had crucified three small
frogs since dawn and wrestled successfully with a big
Jacob eel which had him in a leglock until he scissored
it into submission and wound it down his throat in
gagging stages. He froze as the mizzen star grazed past
him, and the horse sensed him among the reeds but
saw only a hiccuping bullrush with eyes. Later the
bittern would fly in his heavy direct manner as though

132

wired through the air with his ski-stick legs trailing
and his trussed neck reined back between his sedge-
coloured wings to the bogs of the upper lake, his eye
fiercely targetting his landing. Here he would spend
his day in whistling gnat silence, reedy concentration
and occasional murder.

Miceal was on the road to Coolnay, wearing his good
tweed jacket and the Ma's cobbled white jersey kept
for Christmas and best. He smelled fiercely against the
moths like a tomcat under chloroform. Bloody boots,
but what the hell can you do else in this place with
water on all sides, as well as it dropping from the sky
like a sieve, clouds and everything sifting through on to
a land no better than a squashed cabbage, and as
strained full of bog-holes as a colander. Jesus, this
jersey's strong. The old ram's looking round to see is
it King Puck on the road behind him and if it is, me
bonny boyo, we'll see who it is has the better horns,
you, me or the Devil.

The white-headed collie needled behind the flock,
nipping a running stitch here and there at the sides to
keep it together, the white loom of fleeces clicking on
the road. The mushroom tents along the dunes had
most of them fallen in wet fungoid heaps, and people
everywhere were drying out and packing up, unable to
trust in the turncoat weather. One by one most of the
caravans snailed away up the main road to the ferry.
Miceal saw the blue and yellow tent was now behind
the ring of furze some way off the strand, the shabby
smaller one beside it. He wondered when they had
moved, in the morning or last night when Paudi was
with them. He would surely have got them away there

by dark, but then so few knew what the Atlantic could throw at Aranchilla. Where most places might have a cat's spat, the old giant out there had a lion by the tail which clawed a footing on the island at every swing. Small wonder that the barnacles and the cabins stuck so hard to the rock, and we become God knows as salt and stubborn ourselves as the adamant limpet. And like them we shrivel if we're chipped from our parent stone.

There's a thing, to be turned inside out by the wind like a squid's stomach and call it fun, those campers. Still, you could drown in Guinness and be happy. Paudi had come in late. What the hell does he find to do. Miceal grinned. The milk was as turned as Father Muldoon's face at the end of Lent. Paudi would have a fine chase after the old one this morning for a drop of the fresh, and she with a sore tit ready to give him a boost back to his bloody boats he needn't stop to catch a train.

Where would she be now, how would she be looking. Waiting by a stone on the brow of the Bull, or standing in a green place. Or would he be there first. Maybe she would not come. *Ah God woman, be there.*

He chivied the sheep up the narrow track over the bog, sliced on every side like black bread, the narrow donkey-brown peat nuggets in humped piles like asses with their backs to the wind. Until you got to the grass at the Bull's knees where his green dewlaps folded against the harsh heather, it was black, a black country riven with bronze water. He had thought this must be the place where the black king and his horses came up out of the earth to claim summer's daughter.

The girl would have dropped her flowers like this one. Some child's been here. And the wheel tracks going down into the darkness. Ye're a gormless romancer, Mick. No chariot's been here since the days of Fergus, and Ma Gallagher's ass is no black charger with eyes of fire. Which is no bad description of the old one herself. The devil couldn't curb that one with any known bridle.

The sheep bucketted the last few yards and fanned out in wool fingers as they reached the short grass at the Bull's feet, hurrying and snatching quick bites as though shredding a green newspaper as they ran. The old ram pushed the prow of his horns through them until he reached the first of the rocks, where he hitched himself up and down against it on an abacus of lice. Surely she wouldn't be at the top yet. She could come up from the strand, but you'd need to be like the sheep on the narrow wet track, and that mostly rock. Watch the sheep, man. Go easy, you're hareing about like a dog after rabbits. The collie bristled and ran forward round the rock. Miceal's stomach lurched. He felt tight in the head, as though someone was knitting a net of string round it. When Paddy Mooney stepped out with his pipe going he stifled the sudden gladness he felt must be shouting out of him, and struggled with the great turbot of disappointment that fell wetly on him. He felt he must have his mouth open, fish-like and witless. 'Tis a fine day, Miceal. Ye're looking well. God choke the old fool, he'll be on this half-hour now. Ye would not be seeing a black and a brown lamb, now. I've lost them these past two weeks, Miceal, and now I wouldn't be worrying but they were the young one's, Eileen, ye know. And she's breaking her heart for them. They were the only ones born this year like it and she dotes on them. 'Tis the dogs I'm afraid of, Miceal.

135

They run all over the island with the people coming and going all ways. Would ye be looking for anything yerself. Please God, all's well with ye, Miceal. It's a wonder the old crow doesn't go up like a bit of dry whin with all that smoke under his thatch. Caw caw and half of it coughing like an old ram with the hoose. No, I have not Paddy. No, not at all. Aye, 'tis a fine day, a fine day. God be praised. So it is. Aye, so 'tis. No, no. Hard man yerself. Ah, now. 'Tis well yeh looking too. Sure, we're none of us getting any younger. Well now, to tell you the truth I was looking for the old bit of a stick I had with me the last time I was hereabouts. A grand bit of a thorn, and I mislaid it someplace. Mother, will ye turn the deaf ear, 'tis only the western half of a lie. Aye, I'll be getting along, man. All the best now, Paddy. *Ah, will ye feck off, man.* Aye, all the best. Say I was asking for them. Please God the old whore doesn't stand around and spy her. If we're seen together there'll be enough gas to take the earth up like a balloon, and hell up by the roots with it. And the devil the only one with a parachute, shouting O me boys, where the hell do I go now.

♘

Do you always talk to yourself, Miceal. If you could have seen your face change when Mr. Mooney arrived. Selene was sitting on a folded coat on a flat rock. O yes, we had a long talk. I think he wondered what I was doing, and I said I was watching the falcons up here. O yellow-eyed hawk of the mind, but he didn't know Yeats, though he listened politely. Ye're from the tents, he said, and made it sound like unpredictable Egyptian Royalty on a lion hunt. Ye'll be wanting lions now, mam, is it. Well now, I think we've a couple left

136

behind Mr. Feeney's. Anything to oblige ye, mam. Sure, we like to see ye enjoy yerselves in a bit of a chase if ye've a mind to it. Do you stand here, mam, lady, yer honour, and I'll be after seeing if we can give them a bit of a dig so they'll be all ready for the chasing, and well roused for the devouring of ye all, ye mad whoring, uncatholic majesties. Miceal had to laugh. It was a glorious imitation of poor old Paddy, complete with coughs and the odd spreading grins he made round his pipe like young horses in greeting. Shall we go to the top then, he said, taking out a packet of cigarettes and lighting one. She did not smoke, and walked behind him as they climbed up one of the trickling sheep tracks, crossing the many fast threads of water which spattered down the side of the Bull, cutting veins through the bog on the landward side, and falling onto the strand over the cliff edge. When they reached the sand, they spread out with curious pulses, as though from the Bull's heart, and Selene thought of the southern bull as he stands watching the manoeuvering picador, the red fountain spraying out of his hump, dropping audibly onto the sand, rolling away like spilled rubies. The green hump of Aranchilla's bull was full and hard still, he was untouched by the pic of the centuries, and his neck would never sink in, nor his eye die with the sun. The horses of the sea would never drag him from the white sands with his shuddering teeth and one horn harrowing the patterned circle where Christ and the Devil rode him and *Humanity* was engraved on the magician's sword.

I would not want to see a beast hurt like that, Miceal had said when she told him. They must die, surely, but no one would wish to use an ass so, nor a pig. Aye, we use the knife, but not to cut or torment them first. A sheep may cry to God as well as can a woman. Yeh

137

must be the hard one, Selene, to see such a thing and
not have the heart in yeh turned over for pity.

He touched her hair. Yeh're as black as a Kerry cow
yehself. I've not seen the women wearing their hair this
long before. Here they'd be afraid to, for appearing out
of place, unlike the rest, yeh see. He sank both hands
into his jacket pockets as though afraid of them. *Hell,*
he said to no one. He thought of how they went on in
films. By now he'd have had her pinned like a shorn
ewe and splattering her with fine talk, not sitting like a
bloody heron on a cold day with the ice setting. He
looked unhappily down on his wet boots. Selene saw
the long curve of his eyelashes, unusual on a man, and
wondered if his children would have them. The ledge
of his cheek bones was harsh, like the rock around
them. The big body and the savage yet gentle face, he
didn't know how to use them, nor the pale wolf's eyes
that would throw most women flat on their backs with
one slap. Or would it. What were most women. Selene
did not know. She laid her head carefully against his
shoulder. What are you afraid of, Miceal. His voice
came strange and deep. Nothing that I can think,
except maybe a fall off this height. Are you always so
in fear of the wrath of God. We all walk in fear of
God, woman, but sure we'll not be talking of that now.
There are some things yeh shouldn't be speaking of in
that way.

When her head touched him, it felt as though she had
rubbed fire on him. He itched and sweat crept down his
ribs. God, I smell like a fox he thought angrily. His
hands began to shake and to avoid showing her he

138

settled himself carefully on one elbow, roughly moving
her head. He hoped she'd sit up then. He was annoyed
with himself at the pleasure which ferreted through
him as she opened his coat and leaned against his
chest. She snuffed at his thick jersey, and pulled a face
up at him. You're a powerful man in more ways than
one, Miceal. The moths, he said. What do I smell of
then. Come on, something must be going on in your
fermenting little mind. What did she smell of, this
brown animal. What did girls smell of. Dresses and
scent and hairwash. He considered her. A bit like the
sheep in the hair, everyone did. A nice scent, but that
was the thyme flowers they sat on. She smelt somewhat in the same way as a new book, or new boots, the
shine on her brown skin. God in heaven, what a
question. He sniffed the warmth of her. Yeh smell like
a woman to me, and was amazed at her explosion of
laughter. That's the best compliment I've had in years.
He hadn't recovered from his momentary relaxation
when he felt her hand on the hair of the back of his
neck. He stiffened like a young horse still new to the
bridle as it goes over his head. He could not look at
her. You want me, Miceal, and I'm here. Look at me,
damn you. He spoke stiffly, remembering this was like
when his Ma had slapped his face all those years back,
the tears and the sting and the mouthful of bread he
couldn't swallow for hurt. It's wrong to talk like that,
woman. 'Tis the devil speaking in yeh. *Bloody liar*
said a voice inside him. The voice you heard was like
your own but came somewhere together from your
head and throat speaking into your ears and stomach
at the same time, daft. He tried reason. Look now,
wisha. We're different altogether. Yeh a foreigner and
I know nothing of what you know. We're apart in
everything we do or think of, Selene. And we're not

of the one religion at all. I'm more Catholic than you.
She refused to get annoyed, like a cat being teased by
a warm fire. I was brought up as Greek Orthodox. Balls
to religion. He was miserable. This is a sin, it would
be a sin. It is sin now, your thoughts are steaming
with lovely crackling sin, Miceal, and you well know it.
You're a damn hypocrite. She worried at him like a
terrier after a badger, then oiling like a cat. She upset,
fascinated, confused, delighted and tormented him with
arguments and laughter, and he began to fight her back,
surprised how easy it was. The hours must be flying
he said. And time and the world are ever in flight
and they dance like the waves of the sea. That's not
right, but it sounds better. She sat up, stretching by
curling her spine over like a cat. I've not met a woman
like you. Before. Now she wasn't looking at him, he
watched her hungrily. The bones of her hands and
ankles, her toes crinkling in the mauve thyme sprigs.
He took in her face, new to the landscape, measured
it against the rock, separated it from the land, and her
hair from the sea. When she looked round at him he
didn't shy like a green horse from her eyes, but went
into them hard. She came down on him, stretched herself against him. Her eyes were like one of the deep
bog-holes where bronze goes down into thick black.
In the middle of them she had queer yellow specks,
like the sun, and a grey ring between them and the
pupil. The whites showed very clear, like a peeled egg.
A cold wind touched them both, curling the hair from
her face. The weather sense in him prodded. It's going
to rain. I know, she said. Doesn't it worry you. No. It
began to mist quietly, like someone breathing from the
sea, softly rustling over the rocks. Selene, we'd best be
going. It mists over fast up here, and can be a danger.
Come, up with you. She stood against him, and he

140

put the sides of his jacket instinctively around her
back. The sound of the sea rose up to them and a
hawk screamed below them on the cliff face. Somehow
it was queer the hawk should be below them he thought.
He saw her hair was speckled with the rain like a
starling's feathers, her eyelashes held a pearl on each
one. Selene kissed him, the rain cold on her hand when
she pulled his head down to her. He felt her face wet,
her eyes flinching under the rain. She was warm and the
mist on her wet and salt like the sea. He felt her
tongue on his mouth. *Ah God, woman* he said, and
forgot he worried over how the hell you really kissed
a woman like they did in the films.

He was surprised at her strength. She had pulled him
down with her, and he knelt shivering above her. He
jerked back. Take me, Miceal, love me. No, no. Not
here. Selene. Listen. I love you. Holy Mother, I'm
destroyed. You will be if you never love, Miceal.
You'll be as destroyed as if you'd never been born.
She sounded as though she was cursing him, he
thought. Not here, Selene. Yeh've no thought there
might be someone even now with his eye hung on us
like a Monday wash, yeh don't know this place for the
ones that see all. I tell yeh, now listen. We'll go to the
dance. That's tomorrow night, will yeh come now.
Please. It'll be easier with a few jars. I don't know,
honest to Jesus woman, I don't know where I am at all.

He shook his head against her and the rain. She
thought of the bull when he feels and cares no more
and waits for the sword.

All I've done and thought this day has been a sin.

You've done nothing, don't be so stupid. Miceal. What in the world you'd do if you had I can't imagine. You're roasting like a leg of pork already, and you've only kissed me once. Are you Irish all like this. What the hell happens on your marriage night, if you ever get round to that doubly sinful thought. Now look, that's enough. We mostly marry later here, Selene, and I'd thought of the cousin, Eileen, as you well know. But love, Miceal. You can't have *no love*.

They say it comes later, God willing. I don't know what yeh mean by love. It's mostly talk. The rest is between a man and his wife only. He thought of Paudi, and the talk of some of the lads who'd been with the girls in the summer. They had no trouble with their confessions either, they'd said so. I suppose I'm afraid with yeh, he said, not meaning it. Ah, Miceal. She pulled him down roughly to her and bit him on the tendons of his neck. Remember what I said, love. Never fear love, take it. Take me. He looked down on the sweep of her neck and jaw, her angry eyes. She lifted the thick fallen hair off his face and he kissed her like a hurt beast, shaking and crying against her mouth. Then he lay with his face away from her. He could feel her breasts under his wrist.

She put her bare brown knee over his, spreading her toes against his heavy boot. Her long skirt was dark with rain. I'm no good, Selene. O my dear woman. Miceal, she said. What would your good Father say now. She laughed up into the rain, her hair falling back like a mat of seaweed.

Miceal pushed aside Father Connolly in sorrow, and Father Muldoon in a reeking cloud of black smoke like tyres burning. He thought of the tar-faced ram down the mountainside, and the frosted shape of the mizzen-star like a speckled pebble down with the others

142

by the cat's eye lake below. The collie lay watching them as the rain increased, his ears dripping.

Like his animals, Miceal thought, a woman smells like a warm brown animal too. Strong.

His mind was a hive. He had been so wrought at her kiss that he was now empty and ashamed, yet curiously at peace. He was quiet, withdrawn and saddened in the way when love questions and cannot answer or be answered. He was with a stranger, and yet he knew now the land she was, the lines on her hands paths he could name, the hair lying damp around her ears somehow desperately his. It was like being in a valley you knew well, set in an unknown country. Like that, disturbing. Why was she also as familiar as though he'd put his own coat about her and put her on with it so that she smelled of him as well.

She knew. She kissed him gently. Let's go, we're getting soaked. Damn this eternal Irish rain.

He was silent as they went down in the mist together, and she took his hand. At the bog she went on alone and he stayed with the sheep awhile, drawing and redrawing each moment in his humming mind, colouring the dream with reality, smudging the edges. I'll be along then at six, he had said. I'll be getting the beasts done early. If he wanted, she would go. She did not want the stares and the forced hoofings of the usual Irish gathering, the drink and the sweating, the bawling and din, the disintegration of flesh and spirit which attends the determination to have a good time, and in which the company drowns its inhibitions in the pale and bitter spewing waves of the Powers and Guinness sea.

143

I saw peregrines, she told the others. I watched a pair for hours.

Danny Hennigan and his Ceili Band. The others were surprised when Selene accepted for them when Miceal came to the tent and asked them to the dance. They all walked up together to the dance hall after a quick supper, though Miceal said he'd had a bite and wouldn't eat with them. The weather had cleared again, and the ground dry in the strange way of the island. It might rain for days but drained at once through the peat, and the land held no water for long. The wind had come out of the grey east, a fine weather wind, teazling up the clouds piled like a layer of blankets on the horizon, withdrawing the island into a grey indecision of outlines, the mountains hanging back in the haze, and a smell of sulphur and nostalgia in the air, a curious humming smell of laziness and warmth. Yet in winter this wind would flurry with snow, the sky grey and yellow like a dead toad, a pink sun lurching out of clouds ringing with cold. And the iron smell of the snow. Now the wind promised heat, quiet days passing to gentle evenings, and the assurance of the same to come through nights of hay, serene hills, stone plop of fishes in the lake, night birds calling, in a trance of stars. And the sea asleep at last with its green head on Aranchilla's shoulder.

Selene wore an orange dress patterned with white and black daisies, her hair caught at the front with a topaz clasp. She and Britt were without shoes and her brown

144

arms and legs glowed in the evening sun. Miceal had bought some canvas shoes at the post office that morning, and felt silly and light in the feet like a boy. He felt like running.

They took a short cut over the fast brown river which ran from one lake into the other, down onto the strand and over it into the sea. As they crossed the wide, flat plain towards the dance hall, the mizzen-star and a pale roan mare with her colt burst out of the furze bushes and hacketted towards them. The stallion swung his head low, snaking and snapping behind the mare, his knees high, his tail lashing. He sounds more like a lion than a horse, said Britt. The blue mare propped and kicked back at him viciously, her hind legs occasionally catching him on the chest. He reared when they came near his head, throwing it back out of reach with a squeal, then coming in low at her again. Behind them both the sooty foal galloped anxiously, calling her mother in high concern. There was no stopping the mizzen-star, he attacked and pressed the mare until at last he cornered her, overcame her and, seizing her by the mane, mounted her while the colt watched them anxiously. Good lad. That's the way. The boys shouted ribaldries at them. Eighteen inches of heaven. Jesus, more than that. Henry seized Britt dramatically by the hair. Do you come here often. He shook her. Only in the mating season you should answer, my lamb. I'd forgotten being Swedish you wouldn't know. What would it be in Swedish. Only when my Lapp is full.

When they looked round again, the horses were walking slowly back towards the bushes, nodding and swishing their tails. The mizzen-star stopped to scratch his forehead. He looks like a T'ang horse, Ran said. His head's just like that pink jade Han horse in the

145

British Museum. That really is a fantastic horse, a classic horse. He makes you think of chariots and the moon and centaurs and Diomed. A worshipful beast. For Christ's sake shut up. You'll end up as bad as Lenie. Stew knelt and was bowing up and down at the spotted horse.

Selene walked ahead with Miceal. Do you still want to get up on him he said, for something to say. She surprised him. I've caught him, she said. Many times. But I've nowhere to put the long rope on him and find out if he's broken or not. He's halter broken, but I think not yet backed. She was the brightest thing on Aranchilla he thought. The orange dress seemed on fire, bright as the sun. She walked gracefully, her hair a great dark column down her back. You look like a goddess, he said. Without thought. There's a thing for a good Catholic to say. He dropped a box of matches, and she picked it up with her strong toes, grinning as he shook his head at her with exasperation. I believe you can do anything but fly. And you'd do that as well as the birds if you put your heart to it, I'm thinking. Ah, Miceal. Then I'd be an angel, wouldn't I. And that's impossible. I should hate to be an angel. Think of gadding around in a hospital nightie, and what happens when you moult. She chanted. Modern angels all agree that Stick-It gives your wings that Fixed-On Look, so essential for Next World Living. Harp off to your local store and insist on Stick-It, and see his eyes cloud over at the new You. No more mess and feathers, just Stick-It up your heavenly jumper and Fly, girl, Fly. And by the same makers, Lusto, the Perfect Conditioner for that Shagged-Out-Feeling. If your hus-

146

band is losing his iron content, give him Lusto and see him Wag All Over as he tastes the Real Flavour of Home Made Testicle Jelly. Miceal felt left behind when she went off on one of her imitations. She was so completely unlike any other woman he'd known or dreamed of, and she shocked him out of his island shell so that he felt around for safety like a naked crab, while creased with laughter. Selene, Selene, he said, and shook his head. You have lovely eyes, Miceal. No one would have told you. Quit codding, woman. But he was pleased. She turned on him suddenly, breathless. Let me stay with you, Miceal. We could be happy, and I would even marry you if you wished. You're the sort of man I want. Someone of the earth, like I am, of birds and animals and the dear earth. *Like the little black cat*, he thought. Like the little cat who came to his fire from off the mountain one day, and turned her yellow eyes up at him, rubbing against him. With her claws in his calf and her little pink tongue out. Wisha, he said.

Their entrance caused a stir. There was open-mouthed amazement, withdrawal, giraffe-craning and appraisal. Paudi was hung over a red-haired girl from the North, very sophisticated and at ease amongst what he called the rest of the gombeens. She was hitched up against him as though he was trying her on, and her freckles showed up under the harsh fish-market glare of the unshaded bulbs like the spots on a trout's back. She thought him marvellous, he was surveying the territory for likelier prey over her shoulder. Her possibilities he discovered were firmly encased in unyielding ridges of some sort. Even if you got her that far, it wasn't worth the effort of dismantling the scaffolding and unpacking the goods. She'd be wired together like a box of kippers and always, somewhere, a bloody zip got caught. Her Northern accent was another thing. She hee-hawed at him about his lovely greeyern eyes. The ceili band honked and stamped and battered the dancers in rapid numbers of heavy tempo, commaed with reels and jigs where a few came forward to show their skill, very solemn and rigid, from their red ears to their clenched hands, at attention all over except for the feet swinging and tapping, as though manipulated by someone else with strings. The rest capered madly with pent-up shouts to show weren't the Irish hellers when they really let themselves go, some twisted with such furious concentration they appeared to be going through a religious experience, and some were being sick in corners, calling on the Mother of God between groans and surges of porter. One had already been carried out and lay with his head under a gorse bush, bitterly complaining I see ye there, Paddy Donovan. Why the hell can't ye give a man a hand and not be standing looking like an eejit out of hell. The bush received a thump. Me best friend ye call it, and ye after giving me a dig to shorten me days altogether. He sucked and flapped his punctured hand, crying quietly into a scattering of sheep pellets. A late bee investigated the squashed daisy in his jacket. Mrs. Rafferty, the pride of them all, he sang, squinting down at the bee.

Some of the drunker lads wanted to dance with Selene, but she evaded them. They used archaic and curious words, even in their state, and spoke of honour. They regarded her with a kind of awe, and were stiffly

correct. The girls, after initial hostility, were so overcome by her they drowned her with eyes and talk.
Her beauty they admired wholeheartedly and enviously.
Even in the middle of the Didyesees that chorused like
hounds in covert where they lined one wall the better
to repulse all male contenders. It was obvious Selene
wore no girdle, and they were pretty sure, with their
seagull eyes, that she had no bra on either. How
wonderful by all that's holy, to have a figure like that,
it isn't decent, it's a sin, didyeever and there, now.
Who's she with. I thought Miceal was. Ye never can
tell, with the dark ones. Me mam always said. Ye
remember that film with. Screech, stab, caw, yelp.
Faces bitter and hooded, and some smiled shyly. Miceal
was more conscious of them than Selene. Eileen was
not here, praise God. But then she lived on the southern end of Aranchilla, a long mile past the Bull's head,
working as hard as her mam, the men of the house
only coming back once a year from England. She had
neither the time nor the heart left in her for gallivanting
But you might be sure she'd be told by the little red
fox of some woman's tongue that runs as fast as she
can yap and spreads the same discord in a housefull
of hens or a housefull of women.

He drank heavily, but the drink had little effect, his
mind being still disappointingly sharp. Some older
men were at the bar, only coming so far because there
was one and you might see a bit of fun if you were
lucky. Like the time the four tinker girls came, and
their Pa knocked shite out of them right in the middle
of Sean McNulty and the Wild Colonial Boy. The band
had struck up that grand tune Smash the Windows and

149

d'ye remember that's exactly what we did. And Father Muldoon, God pity him, spouting like a stuck whale in the middle of the consternation. Black as a whale, ye're right there, and it was the Guinness, I'd know it anywhere, inside a man or out. The others waved by the door. We're going now, you two. We'll be along in a minute, Selene nodded. Britt looked pale. The noise surged and booted, and glasses crashed at intervals with attendant hoots and shouts. Let's go, Miceal. He took a long breath and went out in front of her.

They walked along the sands. Miceal was unsteady and Selene pulled his coat off and sat him down on it, curling herself beside him. God it's hot he said, his voice sounding queer to himself. For once it isn't going to rain. Wait there for me, I'm going in for a swim. Selene pulled her hair aside, unfastening the back of her dress. What about you. I can't swim woman, yeh know that. Yeh've a suit under that bit of a dress. He felt for her. She knelt in front of him and pulled the skirt over her head. Her hair fell forward as she laid the dress on his knee. Of course I haven't. She gave a curious chuckle and took his hands, making him feel the warm skin over her ribs. She passed them down over her hips and leaned over him, taking his head between her hands and kissing him fiercely. She was shivering like a horse. She bent above him and her breast touched his mouth. He took her then, willingly yet quickly and furtively, as though he was trying to forget something. She was like the cat from the mountain, she could hurt him too, with her teeth and her claws. He felt he'd died. God in heaven he panted, shaking the sand out of his hair. Lying back, he lit a

150

cigarette and Selene watched the strong face with its hurt eyes in the flame. She got up and walked away from him down into the sea, swimming quietly. A bird flew up off the water by her, and she could see the stars faintly behind the warm weather haze. The island held a curious glow still, as though it was giving out light, an emanation of its own.

When she came back to the dark form on the sand, he reached for her, laying his head gently against her. He could hear the steady beat of her heart through the skin cold against his ear. With an animal's movement he tongued the salt water from her breasts. He said nothing. They were cold from the sea and round under his hands like the glass balls that held the nets. He found her nipples stiff against his lips like the winkles you picked up as a lad, and this surprised him. You thought of women's breasts as lolloppy sort of yokes, not these pointed urgent animal things. So many things he'd had in his hands, had taken away and given life, had planted and reaped and worked at most things of the land and the sea. But they would not be the same now they had held a woman's breasts. And the heat of her. Inside. That was a surprising thing too. All you guessed at and dreamed of was nothing. The pleasure she took with you, you never thought of that. A woman quivered in love as the rabbit kicks at the smack on his neck.

O Selene he said. Selene. God, what was wrong with him, why did he feel. What was it. Gone, not there. He'd had a woman, this woman. A man would die for this one, yet he now felt more alone than ever, that he must be dying in this darkness. She leaned herself against him hard, holding his head to her and tracing her stiff breasts along his cheeks to his mouth. He put one hand over them. I love you, Miceal. Let me come

151

to you. Miceal, take me again. He could see her mouth was harsh with wanting him. He was suddenly free. As though the gin had given. No, Selene he said. I don't want it. Leave me alone woman. Go back now, go away. *Heavenly God Selene, go away and leave me alone.* She crouched down. I cannot be loving yeh. I cannot be doing what you wish. I've gone against myself and broken myself with yeh. Yes, I'm afraid. As yeh say. I was not wanting this love. Her dress lay in front of him on the sand. She took it, holding it against her, looking up at him. You'll die, Miceal, you'll die in your fear and the love of God. She spat at him. Go back then, go back to your cave, to your little death you call your life. Black cat from the mountain he thought. Go back and crawl to your Virgin Mother and your bloody Immaculate Father. It's not the great love now, Selene, is it. I love as I hate, I'm not afraid of either. I could kill you. Why, Miceal. *Why.* I'm sorry, Selene. I'm sorry to have done this like I have. If I take anyone, sure then it's to be one of my own from Aranchilla. Maybe not the love yeh have, but a safe home. No man would feel safe with yeh, Selene. O Miceal, I want you. Don't send me away. I'm good with animals and I can work as well as you. I'm sorry for what I've said. Honestly. I want you. Love. She let the dress fall and reached for him. He was suddenly angry. Yeh'll not have me, by God yeh will not. By the saints woman, yeh will not. I'm the hard man when I want, as hard as that speckled horse you want as well. And yeh'll get neither, I'm telling yeh.

Now, looka. Selene. His voice was softer and he held her gently by the shoulders, his thumbs rounding the smoothness of her bones as he would the grain of his plough's handles. We'd never make any life of it at all, yehself and myself. And yeh know it, truly. Ah, we could love as yeh call it, but it's not right. Not by the Church nor by myself. I'm sorry now for what I've done. And to yehself. I cannot be any different, Selene. All I want is my own heart quiet, my own life. Alone if need be. She bent her head. No woman but yehself will have had so much of me. He shook her gently. Now forget me, woman, and go your ways. He released her and stood up awkwardly. God's blessing on yeh Selene, he said. And be leaving that horse alone. Don't be foolish, he's the hard one like myself. Now, Selene.

His back bristled, he felt she might fly at him as he turned. All the way home he found himself getting heavier and more miserable. He'd been more drunk than he'd thought. What had he said to the girl. What a damned bloody fool he'd been. He'd got out from the teeth. The clever fox. He felt as though part of him had been torn away, left. God, Saturday tomorrow. Father Connolly would hear him. It would help, wash his hands, like Pilate. Only he was the crucified now. O God I'm spent.

The cows breathed heavily at the back of the cabin, and he felt himself crying and he couldn't tell why. I'm murdered, *murdered*. The wild black cat was sitting on the step as he pushed at the door. *God damn the bloody woman* he shouted, and picking it up by the neck and rump flung it down on the step with all his strength. It writhed, soundlessly yowling, its tail flailing like a snake. He gathered it up, feeling sick and desperately sorry, and laid it on the table as he felt for the lamp. Its tail knocked softly as he lit a match. Ah, God help me. It convulsed rapidly, its head drawn back and eyes flickering, a drop of blood coming from one ear. Then it stretched, looked up at him with a curious empty sweetness, and died. There, o there, my poor wee cat, poor wee creature. Miceal was stricken to the bone. He was painfully careful how he laid it outside the cabin, as though trying to make it comfortable mattered deeply. He shut the door and the clock beat at him. He went over to the statue in the window and bent his head on his hands. Mother of God was all he could say. A stupid, bloody bit of plaster and paint. *God damn the whole bloody lot of yeh. Pray and be damned to hell.* He smashed her to powder, and the gold paint off her crown dusted the floor like moths' wings.

He brushed her up with the long heather broom, and flung the bits on to the pile of stones round by the byre. Wouldn't show there. It was only when he got into bed as he was, that he realised what he'd done. He lay sweating, though ice cold. Holy Mary Mother of God, Hail Mary full of grace. He promised her he'u get a new, bigger figure of the Queen of Heaven from the mainland bookshop at Clonport, and maybe the black St. Martin as well. He preferred him, truth to tell. The Queen of Heaven looked always a bit of a Britisher in her crown and red robe. Or a nice blue Mother. With Jesus and a lamb at her feet. And daisies. With stars on her dress. Black and white daisies. All saying love me, *love me*. He began to shake and stutter before falling headlong into a sleep like death. The white-headed collie relaxed slowly and laid his head on his paws.

In the darkness Selene went down into the sea in the orange dress, walking slowly. She swam a few strokes and then turned back. The dress gripped her as she walked back along the sands, her hair heavy and cold on her back like a wet shawl. Out at sea she heard the

154

pumping gasp of a porpoise. A dolphin, she thought. Perhaps he has come from Greece. Perhaps he knew me when I was Demeter.

Father Muldoon laid a strong aniseed trail as he entered Miceal's side of the box. The hounds of hell would be distracted from the poor earthly sinner they coursed, should they ever cross his path, Miceal thought. It masked the stronger spirit with which Father Muldoon had prepared himself for inner strength in dealing with the problems of his errant flock.

Bless me Father for I have sinned. How long is it since yerr last confession. Merciful Jesus, it's the old craw-thumper himself. Where the hell is Father Connolly. A month, Father, maybe two. Humm. Well, tell me yerr sins. I've broken the sixth commandment Father. How. Get the worst over first. Bad thoughts, Father. O my God I'm destroyed. Where the hell's Father Connolly. Is that all, my son. Desires, Father. Yes, son. Have you sought after these desires. Aye, Father. Were yerr alone, or was there someone with ye. There was someone else with me, Father. Did ye touch her, man. I did, Father. Are yerr going to marry her. No, Father. Whaat. God, man, this is no sort of a life to be living. To yield to the temptations and lusts of the flesh and the Devil, to satisfy yerr miserable body to the damnation of yerr immortal soul. Have yeh nothing else to tell me. No, Father. I'm sorry, Father. O and I broke a statue of the Mother of God, Father. Yeh whaat! Had yeh drink taken. Aye, Father I had. May the Lord forgive yeh. Do ye not know ye've crucified him again with yerr sins. Aye, Father. I'm truly sorry, Father. And well yeh may be sorry. And

155

thankful to the Lord's mercy for sparing ye altogether to make this confession. Hell's flames and the furnaces of the Devil are leaping for sinners who would fall so utterly as ye have for the fruits of evil which the Viper himself tempts Man with. In the shape of Eve he comes, to mortify yerr flesh and soul. Aye, and makes it easy for ye with the curse of strong drink. Take the pledge man, take the pledge. Now, is that all ye have to tell me. Aye, Father. Yeh're the fine one to be thinking of pledges. And are ye truly sorry for what ye've done. Truly sorry, Father. Jesus, that damned aniseed. Offer up two rosaries, and be concentrating on the Sorrowful Mysteries and you must have the firm resolution never to ... Our Father ... Holy Mary ... Blessed is the fruit of thy womb. Seat's as hard as sitting on a bloody plough. World without end, Amen. Father Muldoon blew his nose with a roar.

Anyone got any washing while I'm at it. Selene had laid out a patchwork of towels and shirts over the furze bushes, as the tinkers did. How did you get on at the hop. I didn't hear you come back, you must have been late. Ran threw a shirt at her. We walked a while by the sea, but Mike wanted to get back all the time to his beloved cows, so I had a swim and he rushed on home. There was a seal near me, I could see him clearly by the rocks. Funny, there was phosphorescence where he was, you could see him swimming around in it, lit up like a liner, but where I was there was none at all. He looked like something trapped in a bottle of soda water, fantastic. O and a porpoise too, quite near. Ran watched her. Selene, my Grecian ode. That shirt's done you no harm, gentle with the poor creature,

156

woman, you're executing it. I don't know how you get them so filthy. I only did it a day or so ago and now look at the bloody thing. All the Irish are pigs honey. Didn't you know by now. Must you two quarrel all the time. Henry sat down beside Ran, holding a map. Look, let's go tomorrow. The others are with me, and while this bit of good weather lasts. There's miles of bog and open country to go from here, and I don't fancy getting caught out in the gale, which I'm positive will smite us ungodly as soon as we even think of moving. Lenie, do you want to come with us for a last saunter round. We're going up to the Bull's Head. No, I don't think so. I want to wash my hair if we're going tomorrow. O Ran, can I borrow a pair of your jeans later. I want to explore the caves again at low tide. OK, I'll come with you. If you don't object, that is. Let's go this afternoon. I want to lie in the sun as long as possible and dry my hair. Look, I'll get the shopping, I want to get a shampoo anyway. What have we got left, Henry. Practically sweet Fanny Adams. I think I'll write to the good parent and say Dear Father, your son is destitute in the Bog of Allen. Please cough up. And we'll see what manna falls into the stern edifice of Sligo Post Office. If I write now there should be something in by the time we get there, if I can convince Papa that I'm winding my lonely horn on an empty stomach. Ran, old son. Can we get enough together to take us back. There's nothing over this side, but we might catch a bit of the praty digging when we get over near Dublin. There's usually plenty of work around Rush and those places. Well, I'm off. Anyone want anything special. Only you, my georgeous Georgic. Come back to Erin and your Uncle Ran my little fleshpot, and bring me some fags. O, and Lenie. She was someway off. Yes. Bring us back some apples.

157

Comfort me with apples for I'm sick of love. OK,
Solomon. She turned. O, Lenie. Yes. I love you. O
balls. No, apples. He grinned and fell asleep.

Selene went into Mr. Feeney's chaotic museum of
interesting domestic redundancies and edible antiques,
which he gracefully entitled Provisions, which lurked,
piled, hovered, tottered, breathed its last, grew whiskers
or penicillin, or both, maggotted, blossomed, slowly
gathered towards a grand fruition, or quickly died, at
the other end of the Select Bar.

O, and I want about thirty feet of that rope, Mr.
Feeney. That's the best nylon, Miss. Er, Missus. I've
some else there, 'tis rough mind, but then I take it
yeh'll only be wanting it for the tents. Ah, for the
tents. Ah, for the tents. O ho, for the tents. That's a
grand name of butter yeh have. He left a dent on the
butter, patting it on its label, a brown and white cow
on a raging green shamrock. That was a suggestible
butter. Which would agree to all you said. It would
mould itself to your way of thinking. Pity t'was not a
black cow, with horns, a grand little Kerry, now. But
then she'd not have the pink udder to her, and the
pink surely looked the best designed for butter. His
eye exhumed a black thumb of a disheartened banana
which was rotting quietly among the oranges. I see yeh
there, yeh blackguard, by hookey yeh thought old
Smirky was blind, did yeh. Well. Missus. Er Miss.
That'll be all now. Wait till I see. And six makes
twelve. Aye, 'tis a grand day, a grand day so it is,
Missus. Er, Miss. Yeh know what I'd like to be doing
this day, Missus. I'd like to be the oul sun up there
ashining down on all you pretty young ladies on the

158

strand. He must get an eyeful surely, Miss, an eyeful of
the best. No wonder he does be up so bright and early
when he knows yeh takes off most of what yeh does
have on when yeh see him. But twill damp over again
before long, Missus. Er, Miss. That's the way of it
here. Goodbye, now. Goodbye. Farewell, ye young
ladies of Spain. O I had the grand voice, the grand
voice one time. And death to the traitor in the Sevilles.
Out with ye lad. The banana flew out of the bar
window and boomeranged onto the widow Kinch's
washing line. One of those bloody cormorants again,
she said. God have mercy on us.

Ran was still asleep when she returned. The day was
now hot, and he had his old French peasant's hat over
his face. She looked down at him. Ran. Curiously
bitter, curiously affectionate, undemanding, selfish. With
the blue eyes which the Irish had sometimes with black
hair, very clear. Not so pale as Miceal's, which were
like silver. She remembered Java's golden eyes, like a
leopard's, treacherous and intense, the yellow in a kind
of ragged sunburst round the pupil. How he'd wanted
her to live with him in Marseilles. But he'd wanted too
much. To own her. And he'd preferred the warrens of
Marseilles, the intrigue of the streets and cafes, a town
dweller despite his race. He had cursed her. And she
had cursed him back, to his surprise and fear. She
thought of Salud, and smiled.

She left the rucksack filled with shopping inside the
coloured tent, in case of the lurking Irish dog, and laid
Ran's cigarettes and apples beside him. She found a
pair of his faded jeans, and fastened her orange shirt.
She knelt for a moment in the tent, looking down at the
big turquoise ring on her middle finger. It was from
Mongolia, a protection to its wearer against the violence
of horses. She treasured it. She remembered how it had

159

been given to her by an infatuated Russian when she was finishing her studies in Geneva. He had been from the steppes, and he had told her that one day she might have need of it. She thought of his angry cheek bones. The turquoise was rough in the matrix, set in thick silver. She had never taken it off. She picked up the coiled length of rope, stuffed a paper bag full of scraps and pieces of bread, and walked down over the dunes until she was hidden by the bushes. Behind one of them she found the long ash stick that she'd noticed some lad had dropped previously, probably with the sheep. Then she turned away from the sea towards the lower lake where she knew the horses would be grazing in the midday heat, and therefore quiet and lazy. Around her the gorse buzzed and podded.

It was better than she'd hoped. The mizzen-star was resting near the blue mare and her colt. An old dun was beside them, and she was not only easy to catch, but solidly unmoved by anything. They were away from the others and surrounded on three sides by the deep bends of the river. Someone had left the old rusty frame of a harrows at the narrow strip of land leading into the green circle formed by the river's sides. It was exactly what she wanted. Nice, untutored Irish horses, only corn would entice most horses, but here anything was accepted with a long astonished look that you could be so gracious. They watched her approach with interest. She wanted the mare and colt away, the stolid dun as a kind of rampart, a base to work from. With pieces of bread and cabbage she lured the roan and her foal quietly away, though not too quietly so as not to startle the mizzen-star. She had

160

noticed before that the old dun had white scar marks round her forelegs where she'd been hobbled most of her life. She gave her some bread, and quickly tied her legs with the small rope they used to tie one of the tents flat for carrying. She made a noose in one end of the white nylon rope, and carefully coiled the rest round one arm. With her shirt stuffed with bread and some of Ran's apples, she approached the stallion slowly from under the dun's thick yellow neck. It was too hot for them to move fast, and the marbled horse only watched her closely, nodding at the flies. The heat hummed and smelt of horse. She had caught him before, and he was touchy over the head. He had obviously been led but had probably been roughly handled if he was a tinker's animal. She came up to him slowly and offered him the bread, without attempting to catch at him. He ate quickly, fumbling each piece into his teeth and shaking it as though agreeing with her. She continued to feed him quietly, then rubbed his mottled neck and gradually up towards his ears, round his startling white rimmed eyes and still rubbing, slipped the noose over his head. If he had not been quiet she would have had to fasten the rope round his neck from underneath it but he went on eating, and she deftly fixed the rope, still gentling him, down over his cheeks and twice around his muzzle. Now to get Auntie out of the way, so that she could hold him if he played-up badly by taking a turn round the iron frame. Paying out the rope carefully, she pushed and pulled the old dun past the frame where she effectively blocked any escape. The old mare hopped awkwardly and sighed, her drooping lower lip flapping, her ears sagging in the heat, her piggy eyes half closed. Woho my pretty man, wohoo my brave one, my good. There's my brave lad. Gently, gently. Come now. He followed her hesitantly, stepping high like a deer, his head hard carved now, his strange eyes wary. She led him first one way then another and still he followed, his head stiffly poised on his patterned neck. Like that archaic carving of a Greek chariot horse, she thought.

♞

She prepared for trouble as she took the stick off the frame and moved in behind the stallion. He flinched when he felt the ropes on his sides. She tapped the ground behind him and he started away from her, his body sideways. He leaped and faced her each time she closed in behind him, but he had to go on in the circle she intended. The banks of the river ringed them both. Sweating, he began to accept her direction, becoming more fluid and less jerking in his movements, and then she brought him up to her and rewarded him with an apple. He accepted it, watching her carefully. She drove him on the other side, his wild blue eye glittering back at her. She drove him along past the average time for this first submission a horse must accept, until he turned a dark carnelian with sweat and his sides heaved. His tail hung quietly now, and he no longer slashed it when she spoke or touched him. She sent him on and stopped him again and again, until he was glad to rest. Then she brought him into her, hand over hand, and found he was not unused to being handled all over, although he clamped his striped tail down hard when she passed her hand over his rump. He bunched together, curved hard as an armadillo, his spiked mane stiff with sweat. He stamped angrily when she came to his knees and would have bitten her. At the hips he clenched himself and snatched his hindlegs up. He'd not had his legs handled then. Damn. She

162

used the rest of the rope to bring him down, working intensely, both of them now sweating. While he knelt, trussed down like an untidy red and white parcel ready to burst, she handled his forelegs and then allowed him up. He gave her no trouble now. The hindlegs would be different. She brought him down again, and then pulled him over on his side. He struggled for a moment and then gave up with a groan, breathing in deep grunts. She roped all four legs together, and rubbed and patted and gentled him until he was as quiet all over as a satisfied pig. Then on the other side, and she leaned against his back and got on and off him. His eye looked back at her, then closed in the heat. When he got up he left a flattened wet patch where he had lain. Round and round. Up and back. And now he walked beside her well, his great splashed body contained between the stick, a length of wet rope, and her will.

Well done, grandma. Selene untied the old mare, but she wouldn't move and had to be whisked with the stick before she ambled away. The stallion jumped as they passed the frame, and sidled towards where the other horses could be dimly seen, riding above the grey haze like a Chinese painting at the lakeside. But he obeyed Selene, and followed her wearily through the bushes without protest, his eyes looking whitely down on her, his nose wrinkled distastefully and his lips nervously tight. His ears, a black spot on each tip, switched to and from her as she moved, catching and sounding, guiding, questioning, accepting. Then he fluttered down his nostrils. He stopped, lowered his

163

head to rub his bony speckled forehead against his knee, and she knew she had him altogether.

᠊᠊᠊᠊

Ran was finishing an apple when the soft thud of hooves on the turf behind him made him look round. I knew it, I knew it. One day you'll lead a dragon back. Look dear what I found on the rubbish dump. We'll keep him and if St. George doesn't claim him within a week, he's ours. He got up and stretched. My God he's a dream, isn't he. So that's what you've been up to. Ran, will you help me. What for. To break my flaming neck I suppose. Well, what do you want me to do. Help me to back him. If you'll lead him, I'll get up on him. I just want to ride him, that's all. *Please,* Ran. She found he was surprisingly quick and intuitive. The stallion was tired. He made no move as Ran eased her gently on to his back. He crouched slightly, but stepped quietly beside him. They put a thin chain in his mouth, part of a dog lead Ran used to keep his writing together, and the horse mouthed and champed on it, looking like a Parthenon cob with his neck arched and his mouth wide open.

The horse of Selene. Ran looked up at her and patted her knee and the neck of the horse. God bless you both. You're a fine sight together. She rode him about, up and down the dunes and up and back to the main road. He became easier, and began to respond to her legs and to turn and to stop at the chain's pressure. She handled him now very gently, and he began almost indefinably to move under her with enjoyment. His tail lifted imperceptively, and he began to arch and play and step big. He blew vigorously in quick snorts. The heat lessened. Time's getting on, said Ran. The others

164

will be back soon I should think. What time is it. Near
enough six. You look worn out, my girl. Come on
down and let's have a cuppa before they come. By the
way how many of my apples did you swipe for that
great spotted bastard, it's a bloody good job he doesn't
smoke as well. No. I'm going for a last ride, my first
really, before it gets dark. Britt can do supper, I've got
everything. Well, don't go and get killed now, just
when you think everything's alright. Selene turned the
big speckled head and smiled down at him. Death
knows better than to come to me on a horse. As she
rode across the short turf she found the heavy turquoise
ring had cut into her fingers. The blood had dried on
the horse's shoulder, and was the same colour as his
coat where the red frosted and flaked into the sprays
of white on his neck. She turned to look at his rump,
where the black Chinese spots patterned and ran
together as though the Book of Changes lay opened on
the table of his back.

The single main road was empty as they crossed it.
Selene remembered how they had all noticed its difference to the white or blue roads of other places. On
Aranchilla the stones had been taken from the beaches,
and the surface was a mosaic of colours. Amethyst,
carnelian, green marble and porphyry shone out of it
as though an old king's treasure train had leaked along
it. Away tomorrow, and she and Ran would hunt
together for awhile. You walked along a road or rode
upon it, and turned away from it, entered gates and
doors and houses, each opening and closing with a
different sound, and in a different way. So many steps,
so many doors, so many keys, so many entrances and
farewells.

On the white track up the mountain, the stallion dropped his head as it became steeper, picking his way between the bigger stones, and she held on to a lock of his mane as she slid down his working back. The tracks separated like a stony parting on the head of the mountain, and she stopped the horse and looked back down over the island. He waited for her wishes, breathing hard, his ears turned back to her. One of those strange moments came when she and the horse and the island, perhaps the world, became caught in the silence inside a golden bubble, as though suspended in amber. Like the princess in a hundred years of sleep, but the world also sleeping with her; spiders in their webs, corn in the stack, mice, birds in the air, fish asleep in the glass ball of the sea, and men asleep at whatever they did like playing Statues. The Angelus bell cracked the bubble, and the horse rubbed his head, where the unaccustomed rope itched, against his cocked foreleg.

Miceal was stacking oats in one of the upper fields at the mountain's foot. The collie saw them first, and flew like a spark down the stubble rows at them. Then he ran back and sat quickly beside Miceal, shivering, his ears back like pressed leaves. Miceal waited for her to come up to him. She stopped the horse by him. They said nothing. The horse reached out to him and rubbed his head against the rough jacket. Miceal steadied himself. So yeh did it. You knew I would, Miceal. Aye, I was afraid of it. What next is it. You still don't want me. I cannot, Selene. All three were quite still, the horse looking out over the fields. I must be getting on. He was very awkward, though like an animal on its own ground. She sat loosely, and the horse turned his

166

head and shut his eyes. The collie stiffened suddenly, and they heard a man's voice calling Miceal down at the cabin. I'll walk back with yeh, said Miceal. 'Tis the Garda Mulloy. What the hell does he want, now. Licence for the dog or gun, I suppose. His eyes looked at the ground as he walked beside her. Where will yeh go from here. I don't know, Miceal. Yeh'd best not let anyone see yeh on the horse, at least not the tinkers, I'm thinking. I hear they've been looking for him these past weeks, and they'll be here in a day, maybe two. The horse jumped as John Mulloy wheeled his bicycle round the side of the byre, hopping between the stones like someone crossing a bog. Miceal. I will not be stopping. Ah, good evening to ye, Mam. Miceal, there's been complaints and a deal of bother from all quarters. Those bloody horses must go. I'm sorry, Mam. 'Tis the heat. I've got some of the lads going tomorrow, and we'll get them into the pound. Will ye come now, Miceal. Ah, good. Ah, 'tis destroyed I am with the heat. Well now, at eleven then, Miceal. By the pound. O, and bring whatever ropes ye have. By the hookey, Mam. If that isn't the mizzen-star. The weather's griddled me wits, so it has. Well, well, that's a grand stroke of luck indeed. Now Miceal, will ye be after taking the beast in here for the night. That will make our task a great deal the more easy I'm thinking, with that big spotted yoke out of the way. I've never felt easy with him around. See the way he looks on ye, the unlucky eye of him. Mam, I'd say ye're better off him, the devil will be under a hide like that. I wouldn't be getting up on a yoke like that, not for a hundred pounds. That I would not. Ah well, I must be away. 'Tis past time itself and I'm off duty in the hour, praise God. Good luck to ye, Mam. Good luck now, Miceal. He wobbled away down the track, the wheel spitting

167

stones out like teeth. Yeh can tie him in here, I've no place for him loose. Miceal lifted and opened the broken door at the far end of the byre. I'd see you in hell first. He nodded glumly. He'd expected it. But of course that's just where you won't be, will you. She turned the horse, and he spun round feeling her temper in him. Oh no. You'll be sitting on a cloud up there won't you, playing Kevin Barry on your bloody harp and licking St. Patrick's feet or his arse. She kicked the horse hard, and he threw up his head, half trotting, half cantering down the track, not certain of himself or of her, and afraid of the chain in his mouth. Miceal watched them go. The nervous leopard horse and the hair on her flying like a mane itself. He looked down at his hands, smooth from the corn. Her breasts. He walked back heavily up the stubble to shut the gate on the stacks. The cows were coming up from the lake by themselves.

Selene took the horse down onto the strand. Everyone had gone away by now. Sand slippered from his hoofs softly, and he splashed now and again through the creeping fingers of the tide. A raven tumbled down the cliff in front of them like a piece of charred paper blown from a fire. A titter of small waders whirred and dropped and shrilled away again as the horse and his rider paced together at the sea's edge. The stallion stepped steadily, flicking time away. She looked behind them. He had stitched the edges of the island to the sea as far as she could look. The horse with his coat of night and day, carrying his clouds and stars with him.

Under the great black cliff she stopped him, and slid off. She took away the rope and he opened his mouth to let the chain fall out. He was free to go. He laid his head against her and rubbed it, then his hard jaws. She stepped back and he looked surprised, his ears quickly forward. He shook himself and sighed, and looked round down the strand. He turned, looked back at her with one eye, his head high as if he expected to be checked. He rubbed his ears again on his foreleg, then with his head to the ground moved away a few steps, sniffing at the sand. He stood still and searched high down the strand as though he'd peel the skin of darkness away with his sharpened ears. He began to move. A high walk, his tail curving up. He trotted, found it laboured in the sand, and fumbled into a canter. He squealed, knocked the air aside and bit at nothing, twisting and throwing himself against his pleasure of nothing like the salmon through a waterfall, a bird through the net of the wind. Silence like a hound ran behind him, snuffing out the beat of his hoofs, and night closed its wings and settled on the strand.

They left early. Henry and Stew were in front, with Letty and Britt. Ran and Selene followed at a distance, Selene barefoot. Britt's hair blew like a head of bog-cotton, white against the black mountain.

As they went, the mizzen-star and his herd crossed the road in front of them on their way down to the lower lake where they liked to spend the day well away from the islanders. The stallion quickened to a rounded trot, padding across the road and jumping on to the bank's sides. He snaked his head, then wheeled and stopped. He gazed widely at them. As they moved away he blew quietly through his nostrils and lowered his head to snuff and graze, his teeth pincering the short turf.

169

Ran put his arm round Selene and stroked her ear. She wouldn't look back. Farewell, Bucephelas he said. Here endeth the last lesson. Love. Her skirt glowed like a pimpernel on the pale road against the miles of black bog. Then the road hooked her over the last hill like a berry on a goat's horn, and wound into the haze like a cooking eel. Up it again crept a black louse car, sparked and was over, and the road shook like water. Screaming, the windhover hung on his cross of air, the hot tendrils of the haze rising under his fanned tail.

Some miles at sea the Long Man Brannigan slept in the bottom of his currach, his cap shuttering his face, his head stiff-cricked on a rough rope of dreams. Four porpoises and a young one huffed and whistled past the currach swinging light as a gull. They looked at it closely, their round foreheads frilling the water, and humped away into the haze. The Long Man Brannigan felt the currach nod in their wash. Bloody pigs he said through his sleep. No use staying out here with them around and told himself to wake up. When he pulled in the last fathom of his dream, God there's fish here he shouted, and threw his cap off. On each one of the pollack hooks jingled a big golden bream, flashing his red scimitar fins and crying O. Pink and gold, like a good sky, big shining shouts of fat fish, flinging their colours like jewels all over the boat, flapping platefuls of fins and rainbow raging round his boots. *To love and to cherish,* shouted the Long Man Brannigan in a loud voice, *Till death do you part.* And slipped a golden ring of bream on her finger.

Paudi was hunting Americans. The aunt Minna had put him up, clucking and uneasy as a hen with one hatched gosling. No, well, I understand of course,

Paudi. No, Miceal has not been himself at all. At all.
Well, ye'd best come in with us. If only for your dear
Ma's sake, God rest her. Don't be bringing trouble on
us now, Paudi. Scandal I will not be having, God help
us all. God helped her. Paudi left her the most satisfying
contributions towards his keep, squirrelling them in the
Chinese jar marked Ginger, which held tea. She found
it extraordinarily exciting to truffle out a pound note
from among the black leaves, to rescue, just in time,
the fascinating pink cry for help of ten shillings going
down for the last time under the boiling kettle. And
she could *decide*. She could stay the black executioner's
spout, or with a thrill of pleasure, tip the lot over him
and see him floating flat on the soggy surface debris
like a skate on the harbour swell. Paudi placed himself
with strategy, laid his net of charm, and bagged the
squealing Americans like pigs by the hindlegs. Borrow-
ing old Mick Tuohy's horse and cart, he bounced them
around the island, and the money out of their pockets.
He borrowed Jim Donegan's boat and took them fishing, extracting hooks and pound notes effortlessly and
without pain. He sang for them and posed for their
daughters, all squeaks like she-donkeys on heat. They
gobbled his every move with their cameras, and swallowed his tales of giants and mermaids with audible
gulps and Mys. He told them everything they wanted,
and they threw the lovely fish money ecstatically every
time he barked and clapped his flippers or stood on
his storytelling head.

We found it Out of this Wuurld dear, but nart at 'arl
as cheap as we'd supposed. O and my *Dear*, there was
this *haindsome* boy . . . Wusn't he, Homer . . . .

Miceal felt good. The day as fine as a blessing, God be praised. He looked instinctively down to where the two tents had been these many weeks. Gone. Now only the ring of bushes and the green turf. The blue and yellow one had showed up like a child's toy block, a bright square wherever you saw it, even up on the head of the mountain. He wondered where they were now. They had started early. He thought of Selene and her orange dress, then put the thought under his boot like a stone on the track. It was no use thinking now, to let the hawk rattle through the mind's thornbush and catch a thought in her claws. Hawk of the mind, she had said. He was himself again on this path. He drew a long breath into himself, the stones rolling into their places in him, the leaves settling into his mind, the grasses lining his fingers, the whin-chat flickering into his eyes, the ravens falling into his heart. All his being settling and charting itself again, as he was. Before. From his bottom field where the yellow flags crowded the marsh, a lark wound up into his spidery song's flight. God's blessing on the fine day. Who was it stacking in the McCormack's plot by the lake. No one he knew among them looked like her. Was she young or old. Old fashioned in her long grey skirt, her face behind the grey folds of the scarf. She was no stranger to the work, seemingly. He wished he could see her face. It became important. To say Good-day, a fine day now. He wasn't near enough to see her well, but he could call. He felt she wouldn't look up, even if she heard him. It worried him strangely. Yeh worry too much man, yeh'll die at worrying.

Most of the men of the island were down by the stone pound. Some of them were owners of the horses. Some had brought bicycles, twisting about slowly on them as though struggling with the horns of fractious heifers, and Garda Mulloy was coming down the sea-road, hunched over his big paws like a circus bear. The tinkers had not yet come. A pity, as they were fearless and gave good help at these times. Good-day now, Miceal. They must know all about the girl he thought. Someone must have put it round, someone seen her on that damn spot besides John Mulloy, and you can bet his tongue's been slapping like a mackerel's tail. He was glad on an island the men are islanders too. They moved off in the heat, their heavy boots sinking into the sandy turf.

The horses were at the lower lake. They decided it would be best to drive them on to the strand and corner them there under the cliff, a line of men black across the sand and into the sea. It was no point galloping them up and down to try and get them all into the pound together, not with the mizzen-star there as well. He broke away, John. He got away on me in the night. They'd leave him alone, he was the tinkers' worry. Once they were surrounded, the horses always gave up. They were not wild, and gave no trouble once their owners got a rope on them. The white had seemed different, but others had ridden him since seeing the girls on him, and he should give none now. A good day's work would do them all a power of good, lazy bastards. The horses came out of the bushes slowly, and they took them quietly down over the dunes and on to the strand. There the horses suddenly quickened, kicking and squealing, and the mizzen-star plunged and darted around them like a big cock trout. They cantered off down the sands, and the stallion bit and chivvied them from behind. The men ran now to cut them off. The tide was just right for it. It came up to the cliff and in behind the rocks back up the beach, leaving a small circle of firm sand which they had used many times before in trapping cattle or sheep as well as the odd horse. The water was up to their knees as they closed in on the horses, some standing quiet under the cliff, some restless. The mizzen-star stood like a statue, the white over his head and neck like gull splashes on a rock, Miceal thought. He felt the heat blasting down at him off the black cliff face. Like an oven door opening. Near him an artery of water fell on to the sands from a gully in the rocks. In the silence it seemed to repeat certain liquid words down its throat. You heard them, but they went with the water. You couldn't hold them. A hawk screamed sharply above the rock ledges. A yellow shell lay in a green-mouthed pool on a marbled pink rock. He saw and heard everything very clearly, as though they had been cut out of time and he was under a glass with them. He could see *behind* them somehow. The heat was unnerving, as though the green was running through him. He was a veined leaf hanging in the heat. The hawk shrilled again thinly like wire. He came up to the stallion, feeling the rope gritty in his sweating hand. He had to pull his feet out of the wet sand, heavy as a Clydesdale's in the hot boots. The horse still watched him, carved, motionless. Careful now, Miceal, or he'll have yeh guts for garters. Somehow he was Selene's. This horse. He felt he was trespassing, yet with a right. When you stand at someone's back door, and they not in. He shook out the cow's string halter, and slid it up over the queer, still head of the horse. I'd be happier on his other side, he thought. He's the unlucky eye on him. He tightened the knot by the horse's veined cheek. He smells lion hot. God, he knew that woman. He was looking up into the blue eye, and he saw her face and knew her as the horse flung him over with a butt from his bony head. He saw

174

the black circle of men flying like crows at gunshot, the bluestone eye over him hard set like silver. The stars were roaring, he saw them black in the white sky and the sun spinning like an orange pip as the horse cracked him, like an eggshell, against the rock.

The hawk was silent. Someone covered the reddening head with a jacket, and the horses lanced for freedom through the shocked group. The pump of their galloping sifted and died in the still air.

There were those who went away and away down the long strand to bring back a tarred door from a broken cabin, and there were those who remained silently beside the figure in the sand. They would carry Miceal to his home, across the dunes, across the road and up the mountain. And again to his long home within it. A dark procession of men walking up from the sea, and the palette of horses now circled around the ring of the lake. And a pause, an inflection in the wind, an intimation of change came over the day's brightness, a cloud on the heart, a faint breath on the mirror of the sea. It would soon be over, this curious interval of time and weather upon Aranchilla. Summer was leaving, like footsteps going away. For a moment she had looked back, a torn shred of her ragged year caught on a dusty thorn. The men were gone, and the road now had no one upon it. Far out in the Atlantic, relentlessly hunted by the equinox, Autumn was running for Aranchilla, like the red fox with the wind in his brush. And already the year to come spitting upon the anvil of winter.